A Fiery Amish Heart

Monica Marks

Published by Trellis Publishing, 2021.

This is a work of fiction. Similarities to real people, places, or events are entirely coincidental.

A FIERY AMISH HEART

First edition. July 2, 2021.

ISBN: 979-8224116485

Written by Monica Marks.

A FIERY AMISH HEART

MONICA MARKS

A FIERY AMISH HEART

Amos glowered slightly at his son as Joshua hastily glanced at the paged buzzing at his hip.

"Must you carry that with you at all times?" Amos demanded. Joshua ignored him, knowing well that his father was more or less speaking to himself. It was a conversation they had had many times in the past.

"I suppose this means you have to leave again," Amos grumbled and Joshua shot him an apologetic look.

"*Ja*," he conceded, refastening the pager to his trousers. "I will finish painting the fence tomorrow."

"Unless there is another emergency in town," Amos retorted, shaking his head and scratching at his full beard. "I have heard your empty promises before."

Joshua stifled a groan.

"*Daed*, you know that this work is important," he protested. "We discussed my position with the fire department well before I accepted it. We agreed that it was important as much for our community as for the *Englisch*."

He wondered how many more time he and his father would have the very same conversation on the exact same matter.

Amos grimaced, his dark eyes shadowing to a near inky blackness.

"That was before I realized how much you would be neglecting your chores here."

Joshua frowned.

"I do not neglect my chores, *Daed*," he insisted but there was no time to argue with his father. There was an emergency and he was already restricted by using his buggy to attend to it.

"Go," Amos muttered, turning his back toward the fence. "Do what you must."

Joshua gratefully accepted the out and scurried toward the barn to claim the buggy. There was no time to change. If the firehouse had paged him, the situation must be dire. He was the last person they would think to call upon, knowing his inability to arrive quickly. With his heart pounding in anticipation, Joshua guided the horse away from his family's farm and toward town.

He had been a volunteer firefighter with the tiny Middlebury Fire Department for six months, a fact that was proving to be a bone of contention with his family.

It had seemed like a good idea when he had taken the job, a way of showing his support of community but the reality had been a lot more difficult than he had imagined.

And now that it is harvest time and winter is coming, matters are only going to get worse, Joshua thought ruefully. His father was not wrong when he said that Joshua had been somewhat neglecting his chores but it wasn't by design. The fire department simply took up more time than he had expected.

You will just need to figure out a way to balance your day more effectively, he thought ruefully, knowing that there was no real way to do it. How could he know when an emergency would arise after all?

But as he urged the cart closer to town, he could see smoke billowing up even from the distance and shock racked his broad shoulders. He had never seen such a conflagration and as he neared, he could hear the commotion of the townsfolk who watched the burning storefront in horror.

The Balkan Bakery, he realized, jumping from the buggy to approach the fire chief. The others were in the throes of trying to contain the blaze and he barely had time to utter a word before a hose was thrust into his hands. It didn't belong to a truck but a neighboring business and Joshua wasted no time jumping into action, spraying the water toward the still roaring fire.

"What happened?" he yelled to no one in particular as he continued to work but the din was too much and no one answered him.

He had no choice but to focus his attention on the matter. There would be time enough for explanations later.

After what seemed like hours, the flames finally stopped licking at the stone front and the thick smoke seemed to thin somewhat.

Joshua was covered in soot and sweat, his thin shirt drenched and his arm aching from the way he had been holding the hose. At some point, his hat had fallen away but that was the least of his concerns when he lowered the hose in his hands and looked about at the stunned crowd of onlookers.

Instantly, his gaze fell upon the horrified expression of a beautiful girl, her green eyes wide and traumatized as she stood, frozen in place. She shook from head to toe, her arms wrapped around her delicate form.

"Are you injured?" Joshua asked, alarm coloring his words as he dropped the hose and hurried toward her. He looked about for the paramedics but when he looked back she was shaking her head, backing away, her long, dark hair fanning as she spun to leave the scene.

"Miss?" he called out after her. "Do you need to see a doctor?"

But she was already gone, disappeared into the crowd as if she'd never been there and Joshua was left wondering if the Englisch woman had been a ghost.

~ ~ ~

Rachel was still trembling when she stumbled into her house, a few blocks away from the fire on South Main Street. She was finding it difficult to breathe, her legs like rubber as she collapsed onto the sofa.

"Rach? Is that you?"

Fiona appeared in the doorway, wiping her hands on an apron but Rachel barely saw her.

"Oh my God! What happened?" her blonde roommate demanded, hurrying toward Rachel to stare at her with concern in her dark eyes.

"A fire," Rachel managed to choke out. "At the Balkan Bakery."

"Oh no! Was anyone hurt?" Fiona demanded, her brow furrowing. "How bad was it?"

Rachel shook her head, unable to discuss it any more, a thousand terrible memories were washing through her mind, unbidden.

The pain is still too fresh, even after a year. I will never get over my loss, she thought mournfully.

"Oh, honey," Fiona sighed. "You need to breathe. You're white as a sheet."

But it was easier said than done, of course. Fiona didn't understand the devastation that the mere smell of smoke brought to Rachel. It was one of the main reasons she had opted to leave her Amish district in Ohio and move out of state, among the Englisch. Everywhere she looked at home, there was a reminder of her brother, it seemed.

True, she had picked another town close to an Amish district because despite her pain, Rachel still longed for the traditional values of her life in the district but going back...well, it was still too much for her to bear at that moment.

But I can't escape it anywhere I go, it seems, Rachel thought, swallowing a lump in her throat. Idly, she thought about the Amish man she had seen battling the blaze in town. At first, she had thought she was imagining things but through the haze of her fear, she realized that he was very real.

He was trying to be kind to me and I didn't even give him the time of day.

She was embarrassed for how she had reacted but it was too late to do anything about it now.

Maybe I will see him around in town, Rachel thought but she instantly dismissed the thought. The last thing she needed was to grow attached to a man who fought fires in an Amish community.

She had already lost Mark. She would not lose another to the same fate.

~ ~ ~

It took several days to assess the damage that the fire had done to the Balkan Bakery and Joshua found himself in Middlebury every day, helping the department where he could.

The cause of the fire was tragic—a simple oversight in one of the ovens which had spiralled out of control before overtaking the shop. The town rallied together to help the desolate store owners and by the end of the week, they had arranged for an event at the local Methodist church to raise money for the long-time residents and owners of the bakery.

"Will you come, Joshua? I realize it's not really your scene," one of the other volunteers asked. "But it's for a good cause. You know Jack and Jane are good people and they could use all the support they can get."

"Of course," Joshua agreed, knowing that his father would be furious when he had fallen so far behind with his work on the farm but Colin was right—the Johnson's needed their community at a time like that.

Maybe I will try and gather some of the district together to attend also.

Amos, as predicted, had been livid at the suggestion.

"You spend enough time among the Englisch as it is!" he growled. "Now you are neglecting your work to socialize?"

"*Daed*, it isn't a social event—it's charity."

"Your charity starts at home," Amos snapped back. "I cannot stop you if you are determined to go, Josh, but do not expect me to be pleased about it."

Against his better judgement, Joshua decided to ignore his father's veiled warning and attend that Saturday night.

And he was instantly glad he did.

Upon entering the church recreation room, he instantly saw the lovely brunette he had seen at the scene of the fire, earlier in the week.

Joshua would be lying to himself if he said he had not thought about her often since first laying eyes upon her but when he didn't chance upon her again in the week, he considered that she wasn't from town.

He was very relieved to realize he was wrong.

Without thinking about it, Joshua found himself drawn to the wide-eyed girl as she stood alone by the refreshment table.

"Hello," he said quietly. "I am Joshua Miller."

She looked at him with slight surprise but Joshua was happy to note the recognition in her eyes.

"Yes..." she said falteringly. "You were one of the firefighters. I remember you."

A slow smile formed on his lips and he felt his face grow warm.

"I volunteer when they need me," he agreed, his ears honing into her peculiar accent. She wasn't Englisch after all.

The brunette cast him a sidelong look, her body weight shifting slightly as if to turn her back but Joshua didn't want to lose the opportunity to speak with her.

"You're Amish," he stated, matter-of-factly and she whipped her head back toward him, narrowing her eyes.

"I was raised in an Amish district," she conceded, darting her eyes downward. "But I live among the Englisch now."

Joshua was stunned by the revelation. Granted, she wasn't dressed in the traditional homespun clothes of his people nor did she wear a prayer bonnet of any color but to hear she had left her community was shocking to him. Joshua had never known any to ever leave his own district, even if some of his peers had experienced *Rumspringa* longer than others. In the end, everyone opted to follow the ways of the *Ordnung* and have themselves baptized.

"Why?" Joshua asked, his curiosity piqued. "What made you leave?"

The woman's mouth became a fine line and her eyes flashed.

"I would rather not talk about it," she muttered and Joshua realized he was making her uncomfortable.

"*Ja*, of course," he said quickly. "Can I get you some more punch?"

She continued to eye him through her peripheral vision without answering but Joshua reached for the punchbowl anyway.

"You didn't tell me your name," he said, placing a fresh glass in her hand.

"Rachel," she mumbled, seeming pained that she had revealed that much about herself.

"How long have you been in Middlebury?" he asked, determined to keep the conversation flowing.

"Six months."

She wasn't making it easy but even so, Joshua got the sense that she wanted to talk to him.

"And what do you do?"

"There you are!"

A tall, blonde Englisch woman appeared at their side. She cast Joshua a wary look but he recognized her from somewhere.

The women's boutique. She's the owner of the clothing shop a few doors down from the bakery.

"Are you all right, Rachel?"

"Yes," Rachel replied, turning away from Joshua entirely now. "I was thinking about making a donation and going home."

Disappointment flooded Joshua and before he could stop himself, he spoke again.

"May I walk you home?" he volunteered. Both women gaped at him.

"That's not necessary," Rachel began but the blonde nodded vehemently.

"That's a great idea!" she exclaimed. "I promised to stay and help out and it's dark. I would prefer you don't walk home at night."

Rachel scoffed lightly.

"It isn't far," she protested, casting Joshua a side look before looking at her friend imploringly but the blonde shook her head.

"This may not be New York City, Rachel but it isn't the peaceful place you're used to either. I think you forget that sometimes. Please, go with her."

"I have my buggy," Joshua offered. "I can give you a ride."

"Perfect!" Rachel's friend interjected before the brunette could argue. "Then you'll be home in no time and I won't have to worry about you without a cell phone. One of these days, you're going to have to cave on that, Rach—especially if you want to live like one of us."

Rachel gave Joshua a begrudging look and sighed heavily, leaving him to beam at her warmly.

"Fine, Fiona," she sighed. "I'll go with him."

Joshua thought he might burst with happiness.

"Whenever you're ready," he said brightly. He chose to ignore the fact that she was frowning.

That's because she does not know you yet. By the time we part ways, I vow that she'll have a smile on her face.

~ ~ ~

You shouldn't be encouraging him, Rachel thought, gritting her teeth when she heard a knock on the front door. *Nothing can come of this.*

But it was the same mental conversation she'd had a dozen times over the past two weeks and Rachel still hadn't asked Joshua to stop coming around.

She loathed to admit how much she enjoyed his company, his nearness reminding her of all she'd left behind in Ohio.

But she hadn't forgotten how she had lost her brother in that terrible fire a year ago and the idea that she was growing closer to an

Amish man who put himself in harm's way in precisely the same way that her brother had died was too much to bear.

And yet, she couldn't seem to turn Joshua away, not when he persistently came to visit every day after his work was done for the day.

"Rachel! Josh is here!" her roommate yelled. "Are you coming down?"

"I'll be right there," she called back, glancing at her reflection one final time in the mirror. She had been taking more care in her appearance over the past two weeks, despite her false and silent vows to keep Joshua at arm's length.

Why don't you admit that you like him a great deal more than you want to admit?

Swallowing the lump forming in her throat, she hurried down the stairs to greet Joshua who waited patiently for her in the foyer.

"Sorry to keep you," she mumbled and he laughed, eyeing her approvingly.

"You are always worth the wait," he assured her, causing Rachel to blush.

"Don't do anything I wouldn't do!" Fiona laughed as they turned for the door and Rachel's ears stained pink.

"We're just going out to eat," she protested and Fiona chuckled harder.

"I know," she replied. "I was just joking."

Without answering, Rachel followed her new friend out to his buggy and climbed onto the bench at his side.

"No matter how much time goes by, I still get taken aback by the crudeness of the Englisch sometimes," she confessed in a low voice as Joshua steered the buggy away from the front of their shared house.

"Maybe that's a sign that you should return to your roots," Joshua suggested mildly and Rachel bristled. At least once a day, he made some mention about her leaving the community and the words inevitably got her defensive.

"Maybe you're right," she agreed curtly. "I should look into returning to Ohio soon."

Joshua gave her the reaction she was expecting, his face balking at the idea of her leaving.

"T-that's not what I meant," he protested.

And what do you mean? That I should come back to your district with you and wait anxiously by the door when you are called away to deal with fires? No, I have already done that. I have no interest in doing it again.

"I upset you," Joshua sighed. "I'm sorry."

"*Nee*," she countered. "I just wish you would not constantly ask me about returning to the community."

He tried to smother a smile but she caught it.

"*Wat*?" she demanded. "What's so funny?"

He shrugged nonchalantly, his long, light brown curls touching the broadness of his shoulders.

"You're speaking *Pennsylfannisch Dietsch* a lot now. You didn't before."

She paled, her mouth parting as she stared at him.

"I'm not!" she denied but even as she said it, she realized he was speaking the truth. Joshua's presence had been rubbing off on her and she didn't know how she felt about that.

Unexpectedly, Joshua reached out to pat her hand and Rachel drew back as if he had burned her.

She didn't need to look at his face to know she had hurt his feelings.

"You know, I am not feeling all that well," she said suddenly. "Would you take me back home?"

Flabbergasted, Joshua looked at her, his eyes narrowing.

"I-I didn't mean to upset you!" he said quickly. "I'm sorry."

"It's not you," Rachel told him, dropping her gaze so that he wouldn't see the guilt in her eyes. "It's me."

I should never have let matters get as far as they have.

~ ~ ~

"If you are not fraternizing with the Englisch, you are not here anyway," Amos barked at his son one afternoon, a week after Joshua had last seen Rachel.

"What does that mean, Daed?" Joshua demanded in a tone uncharacteristic of him. But lately, he had been nothing but short tempered and it was clear to everyone around him.

"You know what it means. What is wrong with you these days?"

Joshua didn't meet his father's eyes as he continued to groom the horse. He did know exactly what Amos was talking about but how could Joshua explain it to his father?

Rachel had refused to see him after that day he had abruptly returned her home and no matter how he tried, he couldn't find a moment alone with her.

He was coming to terms with the fact that she wanted to be left alone but it wasn't an easy understanding. Even Fiona had tried to talk some semblance of sense into Rachel whose actions made little sense to him.

"I don't think she likes the reminder of home," Fiona offered lamely one day when Rachel again ignored his request to be seen.

"That's ridiculous!" Joshua snapped. "She moved to an Amish town. She misses her home or else she wouldn't be here!"

But nothing he said or did would make her appear and Joshua knew he needed to stop trying. Instead, he threw himself back into the farm, winterizing it as the last harvest was collected and permitting the cold to seep into his bones and to his very core.

It was bound to be the chilliest winter yet, even if the snow had yet to fly.

"Joshua! I asked you a question!" Amos growled, bringing him back to the present. "What is the matter with you?"

"*Nix!*" Joshua yelled back indignantly. "Leave me be, *Daed*. I have work to do, don't I?"

Amos stared at his usually mild-mannered son in shock before turning and sauntering away, seeming hurt by the words.

Shame flooded Joshua and he wanted to call out to his father, asking him to forgive his rudeness but he couldn't bring himself to do that. He was far too consumed in his own woe to make amends in those moments.

It's his own fault for bothering me, Joshua thought defensively. *I am allowed to be quiet and mind my own space.*

He finished brushing out the gleaming brown mare before returning the tools to the barn. He stood outside the stables, looking at the sun setting over the horizon. The days were so much shorter now and seeing the sunset only sent another pang of misery through him.

Rachel loves the sunsets. She must really enjoy these shorter days.

He wondered if he should try to see her again that night but he forced himself to be rational. He knew he couldn't force her to entertain him, no matter how many times he went to her house unannounced and uninvited.

With a sigh, he patted his filthy hands against his work trousers and adjusted his suspenders, heading toward the house. His mother and sisters would have supper ready soon and that weekend was theirs to host worship.

At least there is always work to be done, he thought with some bitterness.

As he made his way up the steps and onto the porch, a terrible crashing noise made him freeze.

What in Gotte's name was that?

The frozen shock wore off as quickly as it had come and Joshua flew into the house to identify the sound as fast as his legs could carry him.

His feet touched over the threshold and he heard Maria's voice ring out, the panic clear.

"*DAED! DAED*, WAKE UP!" his sister howled.

In seconds, Joshua was in the dining room. A plate lay broken in half a dozen pieces next to an overturned chair. His mother hovered over her husband's lifeless body, her complexion nearly opaque as his sisters gawked in horror.

"What happened?" Joshua cried, striding forward in three steps to meet his father.

"H-he just collapsed! He sat down in his chair and just…" Edith couldn't speak anymore.

"Go call on Eli Bontrager!" Joshua screamed, dropping to his knees as he pressed his ear to his father's chest. "Edith, go now!"

But his sisters seemed statues, his mother unmoving as if time had stopped moving for everyone but Joshua.

"Call on the doctor!" Joshua ordered again but this time, his voice was barely a whisper. He couldn't make out the faintest beat of a heart as he struggled to listen.

"GO!" he howled, slamming his fists against Amos' chest. "GO NOW!"

A blanketed haze fell over his eyes as he tried to remember any first aid he had acquired over the years.

Yet even as he worked and his sisters rushed off finally to oblige his request, Joshua knew there would be no reprieve for Amos Miller.

Joshua was certain his father was dead.

~ ~ ~

On Sunday morning, Rachel stared at herself in the full-length mirror of her tiny bedroom and grimaced slightly.

This is a terrible idea, she warned herself but that did not get her to change out of the dress she had not seen nor worn since she had first come to Indiana. It was her worship dress from home and like all the other simple garments she had made herself from years past, it had sat in a trunk under her bed until that moment.

Rachel tried to lie to herself and say that she was only going into the district to pay her respects to God but she knew the real reason she was going—she was missing Joshua terribly and she knew that worship in his district was being held at his farm that morning.

"What on earth are you wearing?" Fiona demanded. "Are you going home?"

The shock and worry on her face was almost palpable.

"*Nee*," Rachel laughed nervously. "I'm just going to church services today."

"Which church?" Fiona asked suspiciously. "That's not what you usually wear to Christ's Hands Methodist."

"I'm going to a different church today," Rachel muttered, feeling her fair cheeks stain crimson.

"You're going into the district, aren't you?" Fiona sighed and Rachel met her eyes through the glass, nodding as their gazes locked.

"Does this have anything to do with the fact that Josh has finally given up on trying to see you?" Fiona wanted to know, cocking her head to the side. "Because if you're not interested in him, Rach, you really shouldn't go and give him false hope."

Shame swept through Rachel and she chewed on her lower lip.

"*Ja*," she agreed softly, dropping her eyes. "You're right."

"Really?" Fiona laughed, rolling her eyes. "Or maybe you're interested and just being a stubborn mule about not embracing it. What is it about him that keeps you from letting it happen? You guys have so much in common and you seemed to like him just fine."

Rachel gulped and lowered her stare toward the floor.

"I'm not sure what I want right now," she confessed. "But you're right—I shouldn't see him if I don't know what it is I want."

Fiona chuckled and clucked her tongue as she turned away.

"Seems to me that you do know what you want," she offered as she parted. "The only question is, will you let yourself have it?"

Fiona's words reverberated in her skull long after the blonde had left.

She's right, Rachel thought with some embarrassment. *I've been missing Joshua terribly. I'm not fooling anyone by denying it.*

With renewed vigor, Rachel threw her shoulders back and inhaled deeply.

I am going to find Joshua and apologize for how I've been acting.

~ ~ ~

The air was somber and heavy but Joshua was somewhere else, his mind on the last conversation he'd had with his father before the heart attack which had claimed Amos' life.

Why didn't I call out to him? Why didn't I apologize for my words?

The guilt was defeating and as the neighbors and family gathered in their home, bringing endless platters of food and condolences, Joshua found himself sitting alone in the cold on the front porch.

Both Edith and Maria had tried unsuccessfully to bring him back into the house but Joshua barely acknowledged them.

He was far too consumed with his own grief to think of anything else. In fact, he was so oblivious to his surroundings, he didn't notice a vehicle pulling up along the road until the car stopped almost in front of the house.

Blinking, he stared uncomprehendingly at the female driver, trying to place her face. It wasn't until the passenger side opened that he understood.

Impassively, he stared at Rachel who approached with a tentative smile on her face.

"Am I too late for service?" she asked worriedly, her long skirt swishing at the ankles when she approached.

He didn't speak, his dark eyes staring almost through her and the beam faded slowly from her lips. Nervously, Rachel turned and looked at Fiona who remained in the car but unmoving.

"Joshua?"

"You shouldn't be here," he snapped, his voice almost inaudible. "You aren't part of the community."

The hurt on her face caused him some discomfort but he refused to falter. He didn't need her pity and Joshua was sure she wouldn't have come if she hadn't heard the news.

"I-I came to tell you that I'm sorry, Josh," Rachel said, her words trembling slightly. "I acted foolishly but...but I'd like to start over."

He scoffed and rose to his feet, his eyes narrowed.

"Start over?" he growled. "Tell that to my father."

Without waiting for a response, he stormed back into the house and slammed the door so loudly, the windows on the house shuddered.

She was right to keep me at bay, Joshua thought miserably. *Nothing good came from our short time together. If it wasn't for Rachel, I would have never fought with Daed. No, I don't want to see her again.*

He swallowed the bitterness and pain in his windpipe, racing upstairs to lock himself in his bedroom.

When he looked out the window at the front yard, Rachel and Fiona were gone.

~ ~ ~

The first snow fell but Rachel had been cold for weeks before that. The rebuff that Joshua had delivered her lingered, making her feel sick, regardless of the time which had passed and one week before Christmas, Rachel made a decision.

I am going home to Ohio. Being here is just as painful as being in my own district.

Every day, she half-hoped to encounter Joshua in the street when she was out but he was either deliberately avoiding her or Rachel's timing was terrible.

She lived in a heartbreaking limbo knowing that such a kind, gentle man had been diminished to being so cruel because of her. It was time to pick up the pieces of her heart and move on, a fact she had decided to tell Fiona when her roommate returned home from work that afternoon.

But when Fiona appeared, her face was etched with tension and Rachel didn't have a chance to speak.

"Sit down, Rachel," Fiona ordered her. "I just received some terrible news."

No more bad news, Rachel thought tiredly. *I don't want to hear anymore bad news.*

"I also want to discuss something with you," Rachel told her but Fiona shook her head.

"Me first," the blonde insisted. "Come and sit."

Rachel had no choice but to oblige, sensing that Fiona was in no mood for an argument.

"What's wrong?" Rachel sighed.

"When was the last time you spoke with Josh?"

Rachel blinked at the absurdity of the question.

"Y-you know when," she replied. "The day he told me to leave, the day you took me to the district for worship and he sent me away."

Fiona's jaw tightened and she shook her head.

"That's what I was afraid of," she sighed. Panic filled Rachel and she leaned forward.

"Did something happen to him? Is he all right?"

"Rachel, his father passed away that very weekend. I only heard about it now but the day we went there...they were in mourning, not having church services."

Shock coursed through Rachel's veins and she gawked at her roommate in dismay.

"Why didn't he say anything?" she gasped, unsure of what else to ask. Fiona shrugged her shoulders.

"I don't know," Fiona replied. "He probably had other things on his mind."

Fiona eyed Rachel meaningfully and the brunette blushed furiously at her insensitivity.

"Oh..." she sighed. "And I haven't reached out to him again since that day."

"Maybe it's better that way," Fiona told her. "Maybe he just wants to be alone."

"No," Rachel countered firmly. "He doesn't. No matter what he says, he needs to be around people."

The women looked at one another for a long moment and Rachel exhaled in a whoosh of breath.

"Will you take me to his house again, Fiona?" she asked pleadingly. Fiona raised an eyebrow.

"Do you really think you can handle another rejection, Rachel? You've been down in the dumps for weeks now. I don't want him to put you over the edge."

"I can handle it," she replied firmly.

~ ~ ~

"Josh, you have a visitor," Maria called to him quietly from the doorway. He barely turned to look.

"I'm not interested in seeing anyone," he replied shortly.

"She will not leave until she sees you," Maria said, sounding embarrassed. "I already told her that you wouldn't see her."

Joshua uncurled himself from the fetal position and raised his head from the pillow.

"She?" he echoed and in spite of himself, he felt his heart begin to beat faster.

"Her name is Rachel," Maria offered. "She's very insistent."

Bleary eyed, Joshua sat up, feeling slightly dizzy. How long had he been laying in bed? It felt like days had gone by without him moving and he didn't dare wonder how he must look.

"I'm sorry," he heard Rachel say from the hallway. "But I needed to see you, Joshua."

He expected to be angered by her arrival and Maria gave her a baleful look but Joshua waved her away.

"It's fine, Mari. I'll see her."

Maria cast them a final look before disappearing into the house.

"What are you doing here, Rachel?" he asked gruffly, running his hand over the scruff of his face.

"I came to pay my respects to your father," she replied softly, gently venturing closer. "And tell you how sorry I am I didn't realize he had passed."

He eyed her dubiously.

"You came when died," he reminded her but she shook her head.

"I came for worship. I didn't learn about his passing until today. You misunderstood my appearance that day."

Joshua didn't know what to say.

Does this really change anything? She and I are not well-suited for each other.

"I will leave you alone if that's what you want but I also wanted to tell you a story," Rachel continued. "My brother, Mark, he died in a terrible fire at my family's home."

Joshua stared at her in disbelief.

"I did not know that."

"I didn't tell you because I wanted to keep you at a distance. I wanted to keep everyone at a distance."

Joshua shook his head.

"But why?"

Rachel smiled thinly but it was mirthless and didn't meet her eyes.

"The guilt I felt was insurmountable after he died. We never had a very good relationship and the night he died...I was the one who was supposed to have been in the barn when it went up in flames. I never forgave myself and I felt like no one else forgave me either. That's why I needed to leave my district and start over."

Understand flowed through Joshua but he didn't speak, sensing that she had been holding onto her story for too long.

"I tried to run but you can't escape your own mind, Joshua and you also can't hide from those emotions. All you can do is hope you meet someone who makes you happy enough that you can somehow overcome the grief."

She met his gaze and stepped closer, her hand extended.

"Don't make the same mistake I made, Joshua. Don't run away and hide. Reach out to those of us who love you and let us help you."

Tentatively, she touched his hand, flinching slightly as if she expected him to withdraw but with each word she spoke, Joshua felt his heart grow fuller.

"I understand now why you pushed me away," he breathed, accepting her hand and relief colored her face. "I don't fault you for it."

She nodded and he could plainly see the tears filling her eyes.

"I have been thinking about going back home to my district in Ohio," she confessed and a pang of worry stabbed through Joshua's heart.

"No!" he said before he could stop himself but he wasn't embarrassed by his plea. He had known probably from the moment he had set eyes on her that they were inexplicably drawn together. "Stay here. I can speak to the bishop and see if we can't find you a place to stay in the district until..."

He trailed off, heat coloring his cheeks.

"Until?" Rachel said, her brow furrowing.

"Until we are married."

She gasped and for a moment, Joshua thought he had said too much but her look of surprise melted away into one of joy and Rachel threw her arms around his neck.

"Yes," she whispered, laughing. "I would like that...on one condition."

He pulled back and met her eyes.

"Anything," he agreed.

She looked shamed but she cleared her throat and met his eyes squarely.

"You must stop volunteering at the fire department," she said, blushing as though she knew she was asking him a lot.

"You are already too late," he laughed. "I gave my resignation after my father passed. He didn't like that I worked there."

Rachel exhaled with relief and gave him a kiss on the cheek.

"*Danke*, Joshua," she sighed. "You have given me a great deal of comfort."

He smiled and realized it was the first time he had done that in a long while.

"I suppose that is just one more thing we both have in common then," he replied.

THE CRADLE

PHYLLIS ROGERS

THE CRADLE

The scent of white oak filled the tiny wood shed Samuel Fisher worked in. It was a pleasant herbal-like aroma with nutty overtones. He hand-cut each piece of wood and smoothed them with a wood planer his father and grandfather used before him. He used a lathe to form the spindles, which he fit into the sides of the cradle, one by one.

Samuel took off his black straw hat and wiped the sweat off of his head and face. It had been a grueling two months. It seemed as though the drought had settled and was there to stay. The farm work had become arduous, and between the long days of working in the fields with the blistering heat and taking care of his beloved wife, Hannah, the young man sometimes was overwhelmed. He paused and sighed, concerned. Hannah's pregnancy had proved to be a difficult one. It was the hottest summer on record.

The lack of air conditioning offered little respite for one in such a state. Hannah had lost their first child at only two months. She was much further along this time, and the doctor monitored Hannah and the baby carefully. He told her constantly to take it easy. Thankfully, Hannah's mother, Sarah, was able to help. She and Hannah's father, Jacob, were nearby in the main house, while Samuel and Hannah lived in the smaller cottage which had been built a few feet from the back door.

Samuel returned his attention to the wood. He had cut a white oak tree at the far side of the farm, which spanned seventy-five acres. The graying white bark had V-shaped patches and ridges. The characteristics of the wood blended well with the simple furniture he and his forebears had constructed.

Samuel intended the cradle as a surprise to Hannah. He devoted an hour each afternoon to working on the project and wanted it to be perfect.

There were times he questioned his competency as a husband and father. He had lost his own parents when he was young, and he wasn't really taught what it was to be a man. Hannah's father was the best example he had in that light. He deeply respected Hannah's father as did all the local Amish folk, however, Samuel often felt as though he lived in Jacob's shadow. Jacob seemed to do everything right. He was a loving pillar in their community and often thought of as a leader of sorts. Samuel wasn't sure if he could ever be the man Jacob was.

The cradle was an offering of love and devotion to his wife and unborn child. Samuel sanded the wood down to a smooth, soft finish and laid it carefully on his work table until the next day's work.

"Liebchen," Samuel whispered to Hannah as he went into their tiny cottage and kissed her on the forehead.

She was working on a quilt for the baby. The quilt had larger squares which had alternating white hearts at the centers, and every other square had smaller pastel squares sewn into an "X" shape. The colors used were yellow, blue, pink, and green. Whether Hannah had a baby girl or a baby boy, the quilt would be perfect. She placed the quilt she was piecing together on the table in front of her and turned her attention to Samuel.

"Mann. How did today go?" Hannah inquired.

"The heat is slowing us down," Samuel admitted. "All we can do is pray for rain and for fall to come quickly."

"Yah," Hannah agreed.

Samuel washed up and helped Hannah to her feet as they made their way to the main house for dinner.

"Maemm," the two said to Sarah as they found their way to the dining room table. Jacob joined his family and led them in prayer as they held hands in a circle around the table. They sat and prayed in silence until Jacob said, "Amen."

Sarah prepared a delicious meal, as always. They passed around the shepherd's pie and sauerkraut, while a peach pie awaited them for dessert. Though Sarah loved taking care of her family and preparing meals, it had become a more grueling task recently, given the lack of good, cool air.

The men didn't think about the heat during dinnertime. The long days of hard work kept their appetites going, and Hannah was always hungry these days. She was eating for two now.

***

Jacob arose at 4 a.m. as he often did and sat in his rocking chair as he read his Bible. He searched for answers to assure himself that things would improve, and that the drought would end soon. As head of the house, he felt responsible for his loved ones, but ultimately he knew it was all in God's hands. Still, everyone looked to him to be the calm and rational one in times of trouble. He sought comfort and strength through God in his daily Bible readings. As he finished reading the book of Jeremiah, he joined Sarah in the kitchen as she prepared breakfast.

"Gute Mariye," she greeted him with a smile.

Sarah felt total joy in each day. She arose each morning and saw them as new beginnings full of promise and hope.

"Gute Mariye," Jacob echoed as he hugged her gently, pressing his hollowed cheekbones over hers. His demeanor was always strong, yet gentle.

"Dr. Stotzfus will be coming today to check on our Hannah," Sarah informed Jacob.

"Gut."

Jacob grabbed his hat from the peg near the front door, and rushed out after eating the breakfast Sarah had prepared for him. There was much to be done, and he wanted to make as much progress as possible before the stifling heat set in and slowed them down. He headed towards the barn to milk the cows. Samuel did most of the heavier work on the farm, while Jacob did lighter chores these days. Some days they worked together out in the fields.

It was only six in the morning, but the excess milk had to be delivered to the dumping station by 9 a.m. They kept only enough milk for the day and sold or gave away the rest. The few dollars they earned from the milk and eggs he collected were enough to keep them going, especially since the drought made the harvest so meager.

"That's a girl," he told the first cow as he pulled on its udders. They didn't have modern equipment to milk the cows as some of the locals did. Samuel hadn't given into the temptation to modernize. He gently patted the first cow before going on to the next. He steadfastly ignored the twinge he felt in his chest as he got up.

"It's just a little indigestion," he assured himself. He had eaten too much scrapple for breakfast, he thought as the pain passed. He had more work to do. The animals needed to be fed, and their pens needed to be cleaned.

Though some of the animals had to be sold from time to time, and some had been lost to the heat, there were a good many animals to care for on the farm. There were cows, goats, sheep, and chickens. The chickens laid fewer and fewer eggs during the oppressive heat, which almost didn't justify the cost on feed for them. Jacob remained optimistic and looked for better days. He had run the farm for a long time. He knew the drought would pass and better seasons would come.

***

Hannah arose and prepared for her visit with Dr. Stotzfus. She pulled her long auburn locks back away from her freckled face and fastened her hair into a bun at the back of her head. She then placed her white prayer cap over her head. She was anxious to see what the doctor had to say on his visit with her.

Dr. Stotzfus was a balding man of short stature, but a jovial fellow. He was raised Amish but had left the church to join the military and received his medical training there. When his career in the Army was over, he returned to serve the community as a doctor. He was one of the few in the area who had the modern conveniences of an automobile and a phone. He drove around to all of the homes in the community that needed his services. He faithfully kept watch over Hannah to help prevent another miscarriage.

He carefully examined Hannah and listened to both her and the baby's heartbeats. He took some of her blood with a syringe and did a couple of tests with some small machines he brought to the visit. His jolly demeanor turned to one of concern.

"I'm worried about your sugar levels and the amount of fluid your body is holding, Hannah."

He tried not to sound too alarmed, but Sarah could tell that he was.

"I'm going to check on you three times a week from now on, but in the meantime, I need for you to follow this diet," he said as he handed her a list. "And stay off your feet! You need to elevate your legs and rest."

He pulled Sarah aside and told him that Hannah had pre-gestational diabetes as well as signs of pre-eclampsia. Sarah was familiar with pre-eclampsia as she herself had lost a child due to having the condition. He told her that if Hannah were to get much worse, she'd probably need to be monitored closer to a hospital, so it was of utmost importance that she was taken care of appropriately. He knew Sarah did all of the cooking for Hannah, so he gave her special instructions - lots of meat, vegetables, minimum starches and sugar, and foods that had a lot of iron as Hannah was also anemic. He handed her a bottle of iron pills.

"Denki, doctor," Sarah said as she ushered Dr. Stotzfus to the door and handed him a couple of loaves of bread and some eggs. "Don't worry. I will take care of our Hannah."

Sarah returned to Hannah's side. Hannah grew weary of all the rest time, but she took the doctor's concerns to heart. She didn't want lose this baby too.

"Trust in God and lean not into thy own understanding," Sarah told her. "It will all be okay."

***

Samuel was back in his tiny woodshed working on the cradle. He had meticulously carved a hummingbird into the headboard. He knew Hannah loved hummingbirds, and it was a nice, added touch. He screwed the side panels of the cradle to the headboard and footboard. The bottom panel was secured by joints. He sanded the finish one more time and applied a coat of oil. He decided the color was perfect as it was. The cradle was finished. He looked at the cradle from side to side and top to bottom.

"Gut," he said to himself, satisfied with his work. His next project would be to build a frame swing that he could put the cradle on. He mopped the sweat from his brow.

"Another day," he said. "Another day."

Samuel whistled as he made his way out of the wood shed towards the house. He was happy with his surprise for Hannah. There weren't as many flowers along the path because of the lack of rain, but there was a huge mound of bright yellow Black Eyed Susan flowers. They had black centers and the flower heads were each about four inches across. Hannah had sowed the seeds herself along with many of the other garden flowers on the property. The Black Eyed Susan blooms didn't seem to mind the dry dust as much as the other flowers that had diminished.

Samuel paused to pick a few of the large yellow flowers for Hannah. He loved to make her happy, and there was so little to do that these days. The heat was hard on everyone, but especially hard on Hannah as the idleness proved difficult on her.

"Liebchen," he greeted Hannah as he pecked her dimpled cheek and handed her the flowers.

Hannah's face lit up.

"Denki."

Sarah decided to bring dinner to Hannah and Samuel, in an effort to minimize Hannah's walking. She prepared an iron-rich meal to help with Hannah's anemia – liver pudding, sauerkraut, and shoefly pie. The molasses pie had a lot of iron and would comfort and soothe Hannah's weary body. Hannah was not fond of liver pudding, however, and turned her nose up at the sight of it. She felt bad for doing so as Sarah worked so hard to help them, and Hannah quickly corrected herself.

"Denki, Maemm," Hannah said trying to sound more grateful as she restored her smile.

"I'll get the dishes in the morning," Sarah said on her way out of the cottage.

"You've been coming in a little later these days," Hannah quizzed Samuel.

"Yah," Samuel admitted. "There are a couple of smaller projects on the farm that I've been working on, but I'm almost done. You'll soon have more time to grow tired of me again," he said with a smile as he picked up their dinner plates.

"Never," Hannah said. "I don't know if that could ever happen."

Samuel brought the dishes to the kitchen, and Hannah started to join him. He motioned her back to elevate her legs as the doctor ordered, much to her disappointment.

"I'm so tired of just laying around," she exclaimed.

Hannah was accustomed to hard work. She was bored and restless.

"You won't be laying around for long, liebchen. You'll soon have plenty to do," Samuel promised as he kissed her forehead.

Samuel took the checkerboard from the table in the living area and brought it to Hannah so they could play a game. He was intent on distracting her from her boredom.

"I win again," she said.

"Ah, so you do."

"Perhaps you are letting me win so many games? Could that be, Mann?"

"Nope. You won fair and square."

There had been times Samuel purposefully put little effort out to score a victory, but this was not one of them. He normally gave Hannah a run for her money, but he was tired and ready for bed. He extinguished the oil lamp and lay down next to Hannah.

"Guten Nacht," Samuel said affectionately as he kissed Hannah on the forehead.

"Guten Nacht."

***

Jacob lit the kerosene lamp as he made his way to his rocking chair. Though he had a full night's sleep, he was quite tired and felt somewhat under the weather. He held the Bible he had read from since he was a little boy and faithfully read from its pages. He had drawn strength from the Bible many times in his life, and he had learned the evening before from Sarah of the challenges faced by Hannah and her pregnancy. He had faith that God would see her through this. Everything seemed overwhelming at times – the drought and heat, the farm, Hannah's difficulties – but he knew it would all work out in the end, in God's timing.

It was a day that Samuel and Jacob were to work together in the fields. The fencing needed repair, as some of the animals had made their way out of the property. Sarah packed them a peanut butter sandwich lunch so they wouldn't have to make the long walk in the heat until they were finished for the day.

"Gott be with you," Sarah faithfully told him as she walked him to the door. She sighed as she lost sight of him, knowing the day would not be easy for him. They were not spring chickens anymore, and the heat did not help things. She pulled the crisp white curtains back to usher in the morning sun and went to check on Hannah.

The two men met each other in the pasture. Samuel had filled the wagon with fence posts, slats of wood, nails, hammers and other supplies. He pulled the wagon as they made their way through the farmland. The sun was rising and the widening crystal blue sky offered a panoramic view. The once fertile pasture was becoming more barren, and the cornstalks which grew the feed for the animals were more spindly and parched, but the farm was still a beautiful, peaceful place.

Jacob had worked the land all of his life. It was his gold and in his blood. He couldn't deny it was getting harder and harder. He was thankful to have the help of his son-in-law. He wouldn't have made those past few months without Samuel.

They pounded fence posts into the ground and drove nails where it was needed. There was a lot of fencing to cover. They worked relentlessly to get it all done.

As the day wore on, an orange haze cast itself over the farm and the fields. It was blistering hot in the afternoons. The men took a break under a large tree, which shaded them some from the heat.

"I'm really proud of the work you are doing on the farm," Jacob said to Samuel.

The compliment caught Samuel off guard. He looked up to Jacob and it meant a lot to him that Jacob noticed his efforts.

"Denki, sir," Samuel nodded.

"One day, this will be yours and Hannah's. You've earned it for sure."

Samuel had lost his parents to an accident when he was younger. They were in their buggy on the road when a truck hit them head-on. Samuel was the youngest, and his older siblings raised him with the help of an aunt and uncle who lived nearby. It was a logical choice to live with Hannah's parents on their farm when the invitation was extended as everyone else seemed to have a place, and Hannah's parents needed help on the farm.

The men drank from their thermos bottles and tried to save some water for the walk home. It would seem like a longer stretch since it was later and hotter, and they were more tired. As they made their way back, Jacob's breathing grew labored. He tried to convince himself that it was normal given the circumstances, and he pressed on. He paused a moment and rested his hands above his knees as he tried to catch his breath. His chest felt heavy, and he couldn't speak. He waved at Samuel as he grabbed his chest. Helplessly, Samuel watched Jacob crumble to the ground.

There was nothing Samuel could do. He was in shock. Hannah's father was gone. He felt the weight of the world on his shoulders. He didn't want to have to tell Hannah. This would crush her.

Samuel carried Jacob back home on the empty wagon from which he had dumped the remaining supplies. He tried to wipe the tears which flowed from his face. He needed to be strong for the women.

Sarah looked through the window and saw Samuel pulling the wagon with Jacob stretched across it. She let out a gasp and ran to them. Samuel explained what had happened in a low voice. Sarah allowed herself a moment of grief, but turned her attention to Hannah. How could she tell her in such a fragile state?

"We must be strong for Hannah," Sarah gently ordered Samuel.

He nodded in agreement, wiping away his tears.

***

Funerals were about the only time the small Amish communities stepped away from the tradition of wearing their simple, light colored clothing. The women wore black, and those closest to the family wore it for an extended period of time.

Hundreds of people from around the local Amish communities went to the farm for Jacob's funeral. Hannah's and Samuel's siblings had come out early to set up seating and food areas, from the barn to the house. Jacob's body was placed in a simple pine coffin, which rested in the middle of the living room of his and Sarah's home. People payed their respects and told many stories of Jacob, filled with their fond memories of him, then made their way out where guests visited and ate. A simple spread of cold cuts, cheeses, breads, vegetables, and pies lined the tables. Everyone pitched in and took the burden off of Sarah and Hannah. Hannah was allowed a break from bed rest for the day, but Samuel and Sarah monitored her closely to be sure she didn't overdo it.

When the time came to bury Jacob, a procession formed for the ride out to the nearby cemetery. Samuel helped Hannah and Sarah into their buggy as they led dozens of horses and buggies toward the burial ground. He suppressed his emotions, but Jacob's passing had rattled Samuel, bringing back strong memories of losing his own parents.

The cemetery was a beautiful spot and a weak breeze occasionally blew through the grounds, lending a scant respite from the heat. All of the headstones were plain, unmarked, white stones in keeping with the Amish tradition.

The minister spoke a little, and the ritual concluded with the funeral goers chanting the words to the hymn, "Nearer, My God, to thee":

> "Or if, on joyful wing, cleaving the sky,
> Sun, moon, and stars forgot, upward I fly,
> Still all my song shall be,
> Nearer, my God, to thee;
> Nearer, my God, to thee, nearer to thee!"

***

Two weeks had passed since Jacob's burial. Sarah spoke to Samuel and Hannah during dinner concerning a decision she made.

"It is time for me to live in the cottage and for the two of you to move into the main home. It is as it should be, and your father would want the same thing. It's time for a new generation to make their home here."

It was also Sarah's way of trying to make Samuel feel more comfortable as the new head of the household. The young couple conceded to Sarah's request. There was not much to move as they lived a simple life and did not have many personal belongings. Samuel moved what little there was while Sarah visited with Hannah.

"Maemm, are you sure this is what you want?"

"Of course, my Hannah. This is as it should be. And I will be right at your back door should you need me," she offered with a smile as they held each other's hand.

Sarah was a pillar of strength and faith. She fully believed that everything happened had a reason, and she trusted in God's plan for all things.

After Samuel moved things from one house to the other, there was one last thing to bring into the main house. He felt it was the right time to surprise Hannah with the cradle he made for their baby.

"For you, my liebchen, and our baby."

Hannah's eyes filled with tears. The cradle was more beautiful than she would have hoped for. She realized this was probably what Samuel was doing all those evenings he returned home later than expected.

"It's beautiful. I love it. Denki."

Samuel placed the cradle in their new bedroom off to the side and noticed a chest that was left behind. As he started to carry it out to Sarah's new home, she stopped him.

"It is mostly heirlooms. Some were Hannah's when she was younger, including some clothes that will be perfect for the baby. Leave it here."

Samuel nodded and left the chest in its place. Everything was moved from one house to the other, and Sarah kissed them as she made her way back to her tiny new home, but not before reminding Hannah to rest.

"Remember to take it easy, my Hannah."

"I will, Maemm."

"And I will be sure she does," Samuel promised.

***

Time was getting closer to the baby's arrival. Dr. Stotzfus remained alarmed over a few things concerning Hannah and the baby, but things had not progressed as badly as he had feared. He was more hopeful than he had been that Hannah could safely deliver her child.

Samuel had neighboring helpers on certain days to help with the farm chores, but he handled much of the farm responsibilities on his own. It was Sarah's job to continue looking after Hannah until the baby arrived.

It was August, and there were not too many more hot days left for the Pennsylvania summer. Rain had fallen too infrequently and the crops continued to struggle. Samuel wondered if he should bother planting the winter crops. He was not as confident in his decision making as Jacob always seemed to be. Some of the wheels for the buggy needed to be replaced, the barn was in need of repair, a new well needed to be dug, and more. The canned goods in the cellar were depleted as there was less to preserve. There was so much that needed to be done and not very much money, time, or manpower. Expecting a baby added more to the urgency of it all. He felt responsible for his family and wanted to make the best decisions.

Samuel stopped the plow and grabbed his suspender as he looked out into the fields. Composing himself, he prayed silently:

"Make me the man you intend for me to be. Make me a man that Hannah can be proud of. Help me to be half the man Jacob was. Please look after Hannah and help all to go well with her and the baby. Amen."

He unleashed his burdens to God and felt somewhat better, as he continued plowing the fields. He made his way home, and he saw that Hannah going through the heirloom chest that her mother left behind for them.

"Hannah," he said. "Should you be out of bed?"

"It's only for a little while," she assured him. "I get so tired of doing nothing all day."

Samuel noticed the doll that Hannah was holding. It was a muslin doll with a blue dress and a white pinafore fashioned over the long sleeved underdress. The doll had a black bonnet and no eyes or lips. Hannah had received the doll one Christmas, and it was tucked away once she outgrew it.

She had once asked her father why the doll had no face? Jacob told her it was because everyone looked the same to God, and he loved everyone equally. Jacob had asked Sarah to sew a wooden button at the center of the pinafore, after he had carved an "H" at the center, which stood for "Hannah."

"I had almost forgotten about this doll all these years," Hannah told Samuel as tears flooded her face. Finding the doll had unleashed a wash of memories of her father's kindness and wisdom.

"Do you ever wish our faith allowed us to have photographs, Samuel?"

The question surprised Samuel.

"If we had photographs, it would be something we could remember our loved ones by," she reasoned. "Then I could see my father every day and you could see your parents."

"Perhaps," he told her. "But we can keep our memories of them in our hearts," he told Hannah as he lay his hand over her chest.

"Yah," she agreed as she placed the doll back in the chest.

***

Hannah woke just before daybreak with labor pains. It was not supposed to happen yet. The expected delivery date was still two to three weeks out.

"Bobbel," she yelled and awoke Samuel. "Baby is coming!"

Samuel leapt from the bed and assured Hannah that everything would be ok. He lit the kerosene lamp and told Hannah he was running to the cottage to get Sarah. Deep down, Samuel was frightened. He knew it was too early and with the difficulties she had experienced during the pregnancy, he knew Hannah would be too. He collected himself quickly, because he knew he had to be strong for the women and most especially, Hannah.

Sarah rushed to Hannah's side. Her water had not broken yet, and Hannah's contractions were still far enough apart to get help, Sarah hoped. Sarah had assisted in home births before, but she didn't want to take a chance with Hannah.

"Go, as fast as you can and get Dr. Stotzfus," she quietly told Samuel. "But first, put a pot of water boiling on the woodstove."

Dr. Stotzfus lived three miles away and whether Samuel ran or took the buggy, it would take him about a half hour to reach Dr. Stotzfus. At least with a car, it would only take Dr. Stotzfus five minutes to return.

Sarah's attention focused on Hannah. Hannah held her breath out of instinct, but Sarah told her to breathe.

"Slow, deep breaths, my Hannah," she gently ordered.

"I didn't know it could hurt so much, Maemm," Hannah said.

"Of course, it hurts, my Hannah. But when it's all over with, you will quickly forget the pain," Sarah promised.

Hannah was supine on the bed. Sarah had learned through many births this position was okay until the birth pains got closer. Then, Hannah would have to sit up.

The contractions soon grew closer, three minutes apart. Sarah figured Hannah was mostly dilated, but her water still had not broken. This worried Sarah. She knew the water should have broken by now. She hoped Samuel would soon arrive with Dr. Stotzfus.

Hannah's breathing quickened, and she panted furiously, while sweat poured from her face. Sarah grabbed a towel and dipped it in cool water, as she gently dabbed the damp towel over Hannah's face.

"You are doing well. You are doing well, my brave Hannah. Just try to slow your breathing down a little bit," Sarah requested.

At that moment, Hannah's water broke, and the labor pains were very close together. The baby began to crown, and Sarah knew it would not be long before the baby would be born.

"Slow, deep breath, then one big push," Sarah told Hannah.

Hannah pushed hard and let out a scream as the baby made its entrance into the world. Samuel and Dr. Dr. Stotzfus entered

the room just as it happened. They rushed to Hannah's side, and after a quick check, Dr. Stotzfus assured everyone that both Hannah and baby were okay.

"Looks like you two ladies didn't need me after all," Dr. Stotzfus chuckled.

"Hannah and Samuel – you have a little baby girl," Dr. Stotzfus announced as he wiped the baby clean and cut the umbilical cord. Sarah wrapped the baby in a blanket and handed her to Hannah.

"Now you will know what it's like to love someone more than anything else in the world," she told Hannah.

Samuel and Sarah sat on either side of Hannah, proudly smiling from ear to ear at the events of the morning. The sun was rising, the birds were trilling their songs, and a new life had come into the world.

"What shall we name her?" Samuel asked.

"How about Ruth?" Sarah nudged. "After your mother, Samuel."

Samuel had no words. He was twelve when he lost his mother, and he couldn't think of a more perfect way to honor her.

"Ruth, it is." Samuel and Hannah were both touched by Sarah's thoughtfulness.

Samuel went to the heirloom chest and retrieved the doll that was Hannah's when she was a little girl. Since they had a little girl, it was fitting for it to be handed down to baby Ruth. Hannah agreed and the doll would stay with baby Ruth in her cradle until she was old enough to play with it.

***

Baby Ruth was growing and healthy. Days were more normal at the Fisher farm. Hannah was able to help her mother with chores to help keep the homestead going, and Samuel was busy working the farm and planting crops. The days were getting cooler, but rain was still scarce and threatening production of the crops.

Hannah became more concerned that Samuel wasn't being decisive enough about the problems that plagued the farm. She worried more about things now that she was a mother.

"Maemm," she told her mom. "We have very few canned goods left, and I think Samuel could use help on the farm, but he insists on doing it all."

They always had a bounty of jars filling the cellar. They had canned most of their vegetables, and fruits from their trees, as well as some of the meat from their animals. They didn't have a freezer as some of the neighbors did. So they relied on the food they produced and preserved to survive, but the months of the drought affected their stock.

"Not to worry, Hannah," her mother told her. "God always provides."

"But Daat wouldn't have let things get to this place," Hannah responded.

Sarah raised her eyebrows in surprise. "Patience! It will all happen in good time. Your father had years of experience. Samuel is just learning to be his own man, and he didn't have always have a father to teach him. Give him time and trust your husband and God."

"I will try," Hannah agreed.

The women continued their Saturday work. It was the day of the week when they dusted all of the furniture and mopped all of the wood floors. It was a tradition they did together, both helping the other with their houses.

Later in the evening, Sarah told the young couple that they should devote time to each other alone, and she would watch baby Ruth. It had been a while since the young couple had spent some time together, and Sarah hoped the evening together would be good for them. She didn't mind the extra time with her granddaughter either.

Samuel had a surprise for Hannah. He had waited for a moment such as this. He lured her into the pasture, where he had nailed sheets between two trees. He parked the buggy out in front of the sheets, and there was a projector that he rigged to a car battery. He had found the items in a junk heap in the barn. He played Charlie Chaplin's film, "The Kid", over the projector and handed Hannah a paper bag filled with popcorn.

Hannah had only been to the picture show one time during Rumspringa when she was a teenager. During that time in her adolescence, she was permitted to spend the weekend at a cousin's house, whose family was part of a more liberal Mennonite community. There, she had watched "The Wizard of Oz." She had been amused, then, at the idea that Dorothy would laugh at the two men below in the boat as she was hurled into the tornado. She couldn't deny the movie was entertaining.

"Samuel, should we..." She was unsure of doing this. She was always taught to follow the Amish customs, and many didn't agree with the idea of watching films.

"I think it's okay. Don't worry," he told her.

Apprehension gave way to laughter as they watched the silent film star and his slapstick antics come alive on the makeshift screen.

The young parents settled into one another's arms as they watched the movie and ate popcorn. It was the most fun they had in a long time.

The next morning, Hannah went to get baby Ruth from Sarah, and Hannah reluctantly told her mom what happened the night before.

"I know Daed would be so disappointed, and we shouldn't have done that, Maemm, but..."

Sarah laughed and interrupted Hannah before she could finish.

"Where do you think all that stuff came from, dear? Your father did the same thing with me when we were about your age."

Then they both chuckled and made no mention of it again.

***

The holidays were coming up and Samuel continued to feel pressure about the lack of goods and funds for the homestead. He confided in Sarah about his worries. It was not a common thing for an Amish head of household to do, but Samuel felt comfortable speaking to Sarah about it.

"Jacob and I had the same trials and hardships when we were younger," Sarah shared with him.

"How did you get through it?" Samuel listened intently.

"Well, at times Jacob handled things without me knowing what he had done, but I do know that he sold trees off the property. It would tidy us over nicely."

Samuel had not thought of that. Suddenly, he felt a bit of hope for their situation.

He sold a few walnut trees at the far side of the property and received a generous sum. The wood made from the trees was in high demand and yielded a pretty good return. The loss of the trees hardly put a dent in the forested part of their land, and they were left with enough money to make necessary repairs around the farm, as well as fill their cellar until there were better times for the crops. Samuel also purchased a few things that made chores easier around the house and farm.

There was a good bit of money left, and Samuel wanted to bring the family to town to get things they needed. Hannah had gotten into quilting in a big way and decided she wanted to sell her creations, so she needed more supplies. Sarah gave them her blessing, and decided to stay home for the evening.

Samuel parked their horse and buggy along the path of the street as the family strolled the town. Baby Ruth was in a strolling carriage, and Hannah and Samuel pushed her as they enjoyed the sights of the town. It was nice to get away.

Hannah found her way into a shop that offered some beautiful fabric that she would enjoy fashioning some of their wardrobe items with as well as items that were perfect for quilting. She picked a few things out for Sarah as well.

Samuel enjoyed spoiling her that evening. They ended the day at a nice restaurant, which they had not done before as a new family. As they left the restaurant, they saw a flash of light from the corner of their eyes. It was a traveling photographer taking a photograph of a young family.

The flash of light jolted a memory from Hannah's mind. She remembered a time when as a young girl, about five or six, she and her father had come into town just as she had with her little family. She was drawn to the same kind of flash of light and asked her father about it.

He had allowed them to be photographed, and she remembered him placing the picture in a pocket that was on the dress of the muslin doll that had been Hannah's.

She remembered it all so vividly, yet wasn't sure if her memory was playing tricks on her. She picked up the muslin doll from Ruth's stroller where it rested, looking for a pocket.

There it was – a photo of Hannah and her dad. The photograph she once wished she had of her father when he passed away was near her all the while and now in her hands.

Hannah and Samuel smiled as they looked at the picture and read each other's minds. They had their photograph taken, along with baby Ruth, so that she would one day have a memento of their little family. Though they did not go so far as to display it, they could not believe that such a beautiful moment captured in time was truly part of the forbidden tree they had heard of their whole life.

amish awakening

TORI WOODS

45

Hannah stood at the window of her classroom looking out towards the green landscape that stretched out as far as she could see, dark clouds started gathering and was drawing closer with each passing minute. To most those clouds were a sign of new life, but to her it bore nothing but bad memories she simply chose to forget. Father Smith often told her that in order to find peace within herself she would need to make peace with herself, but how could she if it wasn't herself she was angry at? It wasn't her fault that Aaron died.

"Hanna, will you be fine to get home before the storm gets here?" Kemp asked as popping his head in at the class.

Kemp had been a good friend for her, since Aaron's death he had taken it upon himself to be the man of the house, but as Aaron's younger sibling, she felt awkward knowing that he wanted more from her. He may not have said it out loud but his constant fussing over her wellbeing said enough.

"I'll be fine, thank you Kemp, I'm having supper with Father Smith and his family," she said and offered him a friendly smile.

"Of course, well you be careful now," Kemp said and hesitated before turning to leave.

Hannah let out a soft sigh and sent up a silent prayer of thanks. She was growing weary trying to be nice all the time by courteously ignoring Kemp's advances, but some days she itched to just be blatantly rude and tell him to stop trying. But that will cause a few frowns to furrow on the elders' brows. She waited until Kemp was out of sight before she grabbed her basket with her books and left the single structured school building that housed no more than thirty four school children ranging from all ages.

She hurried along the road to get home but the storm was drawing closer faster than expected. Another perfect day ruined, she thought as she treaded ahead, keeping a watchful eye on the clouds rolling in and as the first drops started plummeting down on her she quickened her pace. The sound of rolling thunder droned in her ears and she clutched her basket tighter, but when an automobile pulled up next to her she realized it was not thunder.

"You won't make it far at this pace lieb," the very familiar yet disembodied voice of the driver spoke from inside the car.

"Lieb? It is a bad habit making such a personal reference to complete stranger," she said to the man and stepped closer to get a better look at her assailant or her rescuer.

"Greetings Hannah, it's been a long time."

Hannah froze; it was Mason who sat before her as big as life, in an automobile of all things. The last time she had seen him was when she was just seventeen. He had always been the black sheep in the community, disobeying so many of the rules, that by the time he turned eighteen he decided to venture into the great big modern world, and disappeared from her life.

"Mason Smith," she said and smiled, "you have not changed one bit."

He threw his head back and laughed, "In this light you cannot see my grey hairs. Now are you going to walk the rest of the way home, or will you let me take you."

She swayed and looked down at her feet, contemplating a ride. She was sure that it will just loosen a few tongues if she arrived home with him.

"Denki, but I think I will walk, it's not too far now," she declined and stepped away from the automobile, "I'm sure to see you at your father's house?"

Mason smiled and nodded at her, "That depends if my father will welcome me into his house."

"The Prodigal son returns," she said raising her shoulders and tucking them forward as the rain started to pelt down around her, "I'll see you later."

Instead of running along the road, she chose to run across the fields towards her house and away from Mason. Seeing him after all these years should not have caused such a kaleidoscope of butterflies to wreak havoc in her stomach but it has. She had noticed the slight grey hair peppered against his temples and the increased amount of laughing lines that deepened next to his eyes when he smiled. He had also no beard, which meant that he had not yet been wed, but then again, the modern worlds' cultures are far different to their own simple way of life, and the mere thought left her wondering where he had been all these years.

By the time she reached her house, she was completely drenched right through to her undergarments. She suddenly felt nervous to attend supper with the Smiths' but unless she was ill she could not come up with an honest enough excuse as to why she can't attend. She was going to have to just try and act as normal as possible around Mason, that is if his father allows him to sit with them.

Chapter 2

Mason left the community just after his eighteenth birthday, and the day he left, his father told him that he would wait for him. Personally he never thought he would come back here, but life has the tendency to throw curveballs when least expected. And from personal experience the curve balls just keep coming.

He hardly expected to see Hannah, or rather he expected that she would still be here, but he didn't expect their run in with each other to have such an effect on him. Even when he approached her from a distance, his gut told him that it was Hannah walking alongside the road. Call it providence or pure chance, but he would recognize her from every angle simply by the way she walked. She had this distinct way of walking on her toes while hardly moving her arms. Now years after experiencing the modern world, her walk reminded him a ballerina, precise and delicately calculated and all his memories came flooding back.

When she ran across the field he couldn't help but smile, knowing that she too had a moment of dejavu and for a moment he silently wished he never left, but he knew if he did stay it would have been for her only and he simply could not tie himself down to a life of common needs and simplicity, he was too eager to explore the world.

As he pulled up to his fathers' house he looked up at the house, as usual well kept, but a simple uncomplicated structure, like their way of life here in Lancaster. He remembered his life here as if it was yesterday, and although he had an enquiring and curious mind, he had to admit that staying here would have prevented many complications in his life. His cell phone vibrated on his dash but he chose to ignore it, instead he shoved it in the glove compartment and got out of the car.

"Mason!" his mother cried out as she came running down the stairs hugging him tight.

His father stood at the stop of the stairs with his arms crossed and a deadpan expression that would put a corpse to shame, but then again his father was never one to show any emotion unless it was to hand out corporal punishment and of that he had more than his fair share.

"Mamm, it's good to see you," he said and hugged his mother. She had gotten old and although she appeared relaxed he could see that life and labour had taken its toll.

"Mason my son, please come inside, we are so happy to have you here," his mother said excitedly.

"Daed, how are you?" he asked his father boldly.

"We're fine, ya," his father responded flatly and stood aside for him to enter.

Nothing had changed since he initially left for his Rumspringa, which he never returned from, and being back after so many years, was like a time traveling experience.

"Lydia is married now," his mom said as she set a space for him at the dinner table.

"I know, she wrote me."

His mother and father exchanged looks and then went on as if he never said a word.

"She's with child, and the baby should be here within the month or so."

Clearly his father did not approve of his sister writing to him, so instead he smiled, "I will make an effort to congratulate her when I see her."

The awkward silence was followed with a light knock and when he turned around to see who it was, he was pleasantly surprized to find Hannah standing in the doorway.

"Mason, Hannah has dinner with us every Friday evening," his mother said and gestured for Hannah to sit down.

Mason turned to her, "Do you not have a family of your own?"

"Let's say grace," Mason's father interrupted and he immediately could have kicked himself for asking such a personal question. Now that he was back among his family he had to be careful of what he said and how he said things.

They all took hands and while his father said grace, Mason was acutely aware of Hannah's hand in his. He could feel her fingers trembling in his and he smiled. He made her nervous; he could only hope it was the good kind of nervous.

After dinner they all sat at the table while Hannah and Mrs Smith gathered the dishes and took it to the kitchen.

"How long are you planning on visiting?" Mason's father asked.

"Not sure, at the moment it's indefinitely."

A loud crash sounded from the kitchen, and his father's intense gaze held his.

"Indefinitely is a long time."

"Depending on the inevitability of it," Mason said.

"You're room is still as it was, your mother never changed it. She waited for you."

"At least someone did."

He held his father's gaze and then stood up and excused himself. He had to give his father time; he had been away for such a long time, with little or no contact. But then again if they were just a little bit more open minded towards the use of modern technology he would have been in constant contact with his family. The few letters he exchanged with his sister was hard enough to keep up with, as it stands, people no longer wrote letters and wasted their time with postage, they e-mailed or chatted to each other.

"I'll get my things from the car," Mason said and excused himself from the table.

Chapter 3

Hannah spent the entire evening seated next to Mason trying her best not to breathe, or inhale the intoxicating smell that filled her nostrils every time he moved. The odd time she visited town she often took a sneaky sniff of the perfumes that were sold, more to remind her just how much power there was in such an evil cheap substance, or so she told herself. But now here next to Mason, the smell turned from offensive to hallucinogenic. Every time she found herself leaning towards him and then she had to recite a bible verse that reminded her of infidelity and the sinful nature of the flesh. I shall not want, she kept saying to herself mentally and when Mrs Smith got up and started to clear the table, she was only too thankful to join her and get away from the magnetic pull that was threatening to ruin her.

That was until she heard Mason mention that his stay was indefinite. That meant she was going to see him every single day until he decides to run away again.

The words came as such a shock that she dropped the plate she was holding. Mrs Smith was quick to bend down and help her pick up the broken pieces.

"He has changed," she said to Hannah, "but he's still my son."

"The world tends to change a person," Hannah whispered and smiled at the older woman with the sad blue eyes.

She remembered the day they realized Mason was not going to come back, his mother was in tears for days, while his father put up this façade of callous indifference. But she knew they missed their son.

"Hannah, you can make him see the truth."

That was a tall order; Hannah thought and tossed the glass into the bin.

"I don't think it is my place to convince him," she said.

"You're right I'm sorry, I just – I don't want him to leave again."

Hannah could understand how Mason's mother must have felt, for someone to leave for such a long time is almost like sending someone off to the beyond. But how was she going to convince him to stay, he had experienced the modern world and drove an automobile not to mention that he used men's perfume. Why would he trade that freedom for this?

"I think I need to head home Mrs Smith, I still have a quilt to finish before Sunday," she said and gathered her coat, "I'll be seeing you."

"Of course dear, but do come around when you want some company."

"I sure will."

Hannah was tucked under her blanket in front of the fireplace and had just started to quilt when there was a slight knock on the door. What a strange time for a visitor, she thought as she went to open the door.

"Mason," she said shocked.

"Hannah, may I come in?"

"I-I don't think it's proper for me to invite you in," she said and reached for her shawl, and then stepped outside, closing the door behind her.

"I understand, I just thought you could use some company," he said with a smile that tugged at the corners of his mouth.

She felt her stomach tumble again and she took a deep steadying breath.

"We can go for a walk," she offered.

"Sure." Mason held out his arm but instead she wrapped her arms around herself.

"Why did you come back?"

"It's a long story."

One he would most likely not want to share with her, but she was curious as to why he was back. What if he was running from the law, she thought slightly panicked, but she couldn't see him to be someone who would use this community as a curtain to hide behind.

"We'll time is what I have. You left here in such a hurry, and now after I don't know even how long, you're back like a ghost from the past."

"Maybe I am a ghost, and I decided to come and haunt you," he said and laughed.

Hannah also laughed and shook her head, "A lot has changed since you left."

"Like what, a few more babies born and a few sad souls sent to the hereafter? Come on Hannah, nothing changes amongst the Amish, you know that."

"Well I got married," she said and when he stopped she turned to look at him.

"And you're here walking with me, what will your husband have to say?"

"He's no longer here; he passed away," and I'm grateful he did, she thought not voicing her true feelings. What would Mason have said if he knew Aaron's true colours?

"So who was he?"

"Who was who?"

"Your husband, who was the lucky guy?"

"Aaron."

An awkward silence settled between them and Hannah bit her lip. Even when they were teenagers, Mason and Aaron always competed to gain her attention. They were the trio of friends who did everything together as kids, and as they got older she always thought she would marry Mason the day they were old enough. But the day Mason left he broke her heart, she waited for him to return but he never did and eventually she gave in and married Aaron, thinking they would have a happy life. But Aaron wasn't the same fun loving boy she knew or maybe he knew all along that he was just a plaster for her broken heart, a replacement for Mason, which is why he was so angry with her all the time.

"Was he good to you?" Mason asked as if he could read her mind.

"He was a good man," she responded averting her eyes.

"That was not my question Hannah," he said and took her by the shoulders, "was he good to you?"

In the moonlight she could see the flecks of silver in his blue eyes, and her heart ached with longing. But this was not right, no matter what her heart and body wanted, in her mind she was determined that she would not lust after another man. Yes she was a widow and yes, she may remarry, but that thought had never crossed her mind. Only now with Mason back she had dabbled with the idea of having her happily ever after, but it was only a dream. Just like the dream she had when she was only sixteen. And from experience all dreams eventually fade and turn into a cruel reality.

She pulled away from him and turned around to head back to the house.

"I do not wish to discuss Aaron with you," she blurted out as she felt tears sting her eyes, "Go home Mason, your mother will be worried about you."

Chapter 4

Mason had this strange feeling that Aaron had turned out to be exactly what he always thought. As young men they both loved Hannah, and although they never showed it in the open there was a sort of rivalry between them. The day he decided to go on a Rumspringa, Aaron had thanked him for leaving, and Mason had felt as if he had betrayed Hannah, but Aaron was also his friend and at the time he figured he'll be the lesser one and allow his friend a fair chance, hoping that Hannah will calm the anger in Aaron. Aaron was your average young man, but he had an angry and cruel disposition, when no-one was watching he was the one who threw stones at new born lambs and shot birds out of the trees with a sling shot, simply for the fun of it. Even his mother had to deal with his insubordination, but in front of the rest of the community he was the son everyone wished for.

Mason felt a cold stab of regret at the thought of Aaron hurting Hannah and knowing that he was indirectly to blame, made him feel sick. He had to find out what she had gone through and try and fix what he had broken, but with the hands of time waiting for no one, he wouldn't even know where to start, or whether it was too late for a new beginning.

He set off after Hannah as she rushed back to the house.

"Hannah wait!" he called but she didn't turn, she just walked straight ahead.

"Hannah!"

"Go home Mason," she said sternly but as she reached for the door handle he placed his hand over hers.

"Did he hurt you?"

He felt her back straighten and her entire body go rigid, her actions confirming his suspicions.

"Oh my god, I'm so sorry," he said and squeezed her shoulder with his other hand.

She turned in his arms and her eyes were cold and hard as she looked at him.

"Do not use the Lords name in vain."

Right, he was among very religious people now, he had to count his words and check his actions all the time.

"I'm sorry, it's a bad habit, but I am truly sorry," he said and then pulled her in to hug her.

"Mason, please," he heard her plead against his chest, "why don't you go back to where you came from?"

Was she so mad at him that she wanted him to leave? He knew he probably didn't deserve her time but surely she could understand that they were all young and he was curious about the world. She could have gone with him when he asked her but she was too scared to set foot outside of this protected cocoon of a life she was too familiar with.

"That's not happening in a hurry sweetheart," he said and tilted her chin up, "I'm here to stay, for a while."

When she looked up at him he was tempted to kiss her, but instead he took a step back.

"I'll be seeing you at Church on Sunday," he said and then tipped his hat and made his way home.

He had to keep reminding himself that life amongst the Amish wasn't anything like the world out there; he had to watch his tongue and try his best not to be tempted by a beautiful woman. As it were, temptation had caused him enough headaches to last him a life time.

He looked at his phone and grimaced. Roxanne had been phoning him non-stop, and he had no desire to return her calls and if he had a penny left he would pay her to go away. She deceived him, made him believe she was in love with him, and then tricked him into making him believe she was with child. He had found out by chance that she was lying to him, and when he did it was the last straw. It was that, which finally made him realize that the world he had chosen to embrace was nothing but a place where people are self-centred and illogical. None of his worldly friends or rather foes knew where he was, he had also turned off his location based service on his phone in case anyone wanted to track him down.

If he was going to make a change and revert back to the old ways of the Amish, he was going to have to consider getting rid of his electronic devices, but he wasn't so sure if he was willing to part with his music. That was the one thing he had grown to enjoy about life on the outside, while here amongst the Amish musical instruments were forbidden.

Chapter 5

A week has passed since Mason's arrival in Lancaster, and Hannah had done everything in her power to avoid him. Not because she disliked him or because she was angry with him, but because he stirred emotions she had completely forgotten about. She spent hours on her knees praying that the Lord take away the feelings that she harboured.

She glanced at herself in the mirror once again and sighed. Why does she even bother about her appearance, it was not like her to be so vain, but she's spent more time in front of the mirror in the past week than she did in her entire life. She rolled her plated hair into a bun and pinned it to her head before putting on her bonnet, she had to get over this stupid notion that there could be anything between her and Mason. He was a confused man with a foot in both worlds, and if he was not able to decide where he belonged how was she going to fit into his world anyway. Tonight she was going to be attending the sing, and she knew for a fact that Mason would be there too. Her stomach tumbled again and she clutched the front of her dress and sighed heavily. The sooner she got this over with the better, but as she exited the house, he was waiting for her. He had borrowed his father's buggy and was even wearing traditional Amish clothes.

"I was about to come and find you," he said and smiled.

"You wouldn't have had to look far."

"Indeed, you look beautiful."

Hannah felt her cheeks flame up and she quickly looked down and cleared her throat. Why after all these years did he still have this effect on her?

"Thank you."

"Can I offer you a ride to the Sing?"

"I was- I was going to take a walk, I enjoy the fresh air," she lied and shifted her weight.

"Are you going to avoid me for the rest of your life?"

"I don't know what you mean."

"You avoided me at church service; you hide in your class room every day. I'm not a bad man Hannah," he said and came to stand before her.

"I'm not avoiding you, I'm a busy woman," and dead scared that the feelings I have will be unrequited, she thought.

"Lying is as great a sin as blasphemy, so why don't you tell me why you are avoiding me?"

Hannah rolled her eyes and stepped past him, "We're going to be late, and I don't have time for idle chit chat."

"We're not going anywhere until you tell me what you are afraid of," he insisted and caught her arm.

She felt a shiver run down her spine as his hand wrapped around her upper arm, and although her sleeve offered some resistance it still felt as if his fingers were touching her bare skin.

Should she tell him what really scared her, and admit to him that she still had feelings for him despite the fact that she had given herself to Aaron all those years ago? Should she tell him how Aaron took his anger outbursts out on her and caused her to lose their child? The day she was promised to Aaron her nightmare started, although she could not deny him physically she hated every intimate moment with him. He took what he wanted when he wanted, and if she wasn't responsive enough he would get physically abusive with her. It took her a good few years to finally get over her fears and make peace with what had happened. The community never spoke a word about it although they all knew, and even when the elders got involved nothing was done.

"Get in the buggy, I'll take you to the sing," he said and led her to the carriage.

"It's not appropriate," she said and tugged her arm free.

"We're adults, not teenagers," he said and then softened his tone, "It's just a ride to my father's house."

She sighed and then got into the buggy, with her hands folded tightly on her lap.

The drive to the sing was cloaked in complete silence, and it felt as if she was suffocating with words that were trying to force their way up in her throat. She had to just get through this evening and keep calm, she kept telling herself, but she knew that it was not going to be that easy. Mason kept looking at her and she could feel his gaze rest on her face.

"Staring at me is not going to change anything," she said and looked directly at him. If he wasn't going to get the hint she was going to have to be honest with him.

He pulled the carriage to a halt and turned to her and unexpectedly cupped her face and pressed his lips against hers. For a moment she froze as his lips pressed against hers, then suddenly that intoxicated musky scent filled her senses. Her defences weakened instantly and she willingly parted her lips, but as his tongue touched hers she pulled away and jumped out of the buggy and ran.

"Lord, forgive me, I have sinned," she prayed and rushed across the field towards the Smiths' house. How could she have been so weak to allow a man to seduce her? But even as guilt flooded her, she kept thinking of his kiss and memories of a long time ago flooded her mind.

The day before he left he had kissed her, not like he kissed her tonight, but it was a kiss that remained with her all these years. A kiss she tucked away in the confines of her mind, and now that, that memory had resurfaced she felt confused and uncertain.

By the time she got to the Sing, Mason's carriage was already there. She composed herself as much as she could before entering the house. He was nowhere to be seen, but the house was full of young eager teenagers, happily singing their songs of worship. Although the event had nothing to do with devotion it was one of the more sociable events, where all the young people normally got to socialize.

She made her way through to the kitchen and joined the older women where they were preparing food.

"Did Mason fetch you?" Mrs Smith asked as she came to stand next to Hannah.

"He did come around, but I walked here instead," she said softly.

"He fancies you Hannah," she said as she moved closer, almost whispering.

"I know, I just don't know if it's appropriate. He hasn't been among us for so long and people will talk."

"You're a widow, Aaron is gone and I can guarantee you that no one will be raising any brows at you."

Hannah sighed, if it wasn't Mason it was his mother, but she knew that someone in the community would have something to say about such a union.

During the sing, Hannah was intensely aware of Mason's presence, but what made it worst was that Kemp was also there, and it suddenly felt like a bad case of dejavu with a very familiar love triangle forming, but Kemp was not aware of Mason's intent. Sooner or later he was going to realize it and then she would be stuck in the middle.

Before the sing was over, she snuck out, hoping that she left undetected, but her luck had run out.

"Hannah," it was Kemp who fell into step beside her, "You're leaving so early, are you not feeling well?"

"Oh no, I'm fine, I'm just a little tired."

She was lying again, she was going to go straight to hell at this rate, she thought to herself.

"Let me get the carriage and I'll take you home."

"No!" she all but shouted, and then toned her voice down, "I mean, no thank you. I'd rather walk."

The look on Kemp's face was one of concern but he didn't push, he simply smiled, "I'll keep you company then."

She was growing weary with this whole avoiding men thing, at this point she felt as if she was a lamb being cornered by a pack of wolves and she hated every minute of it. On the one hand Kemp was a nice man, the complete opposite of Aaron, but he was just too familiar to her. And then there was Mason, who she had feelings for since the age of fourteen. This was all too much.

"Hannah, we've known each other for a long time, and I was thinking we should consider a future together," he said out of the blue.

"Uh-I, I'm not sure I understand?"

"I want to marry you," Kemp said without blinking.

If she had a mouth full of food, she would have choked right this minute. This was a little sudden, and she knew why he had moved so quickly, he must feel threatened with Mason back in town.

"Kemp, you're a wonderful man, but I don't see a future with you, we've had too much history and having been married to Aaron makes it awkward."

"How so?" he asked as he took her hand in his.

She pulled her hand away, "It just does, if I was to marry again, it would be for love and what we have is just a friendship, which I value."

The disappointment on his face saddened her, but she could not lie and pretend that she saw a future with him. She stood and watched as he finally walked away from her before she continued to her house, but as she reached her door, Mason appeared out of the shadows.

"So it's Kemp?" he asked blankly.

"Excuse me?"

"Kemp, you wouldn't even allow me to take you to the sing because you don't want him to see you with me."

"First of all, it is not Kemp, we are just friends and secondly the reason I walked to the sing was because you kissed me. You had no right," she said angrily.

"You enjoyed that kiss as much as I did, why do you deny it?"

Hannah unlocked her door and then turned to Mason, "This is not a forsaken place like the city Mason, we have values, I have values and if you cannot respect that then there is no place for you here."

Mason approached her and stopped so close she could inhale his very breath.

"Do you have feelings for me, because if you don't, I need to know and stop wasting my time."

"Why? It's not as if you're planning on staying here, you'll leave just like you did all those years ago and I'm sorry Mason, but I will not subject myself to such disappointment again."

She didn't wait for his response simply entered the house and shut the door behind her. Regardless of the condition of her heart, she was not going to leave it out in the open to be trampled on again. The ball was in his court now, if he really was interested in her. He would have to prove himself.

Chapter 6

Mason spent a week contemplating his future, and every time he saw Hannah, he was more and more convinced that he would not leave a second time, and after consulting with his father and the other elders, they agreed to baptize him into the church. He may have been gone longer than most, but he was never officially shunned from the community. And regardless of his life style in the city, they opted to overlook his error in judgement.

It was a private affair with only the elders and his close family around to witness the baptism, and once it was over, he decided to go to the school and wait for Hannah. When she exited the school his heart skipped a beat, it was quite strange how his own emotions were suddenly so intensified after the baptism, he had often wondered if this baptism really changed anyone, but now he knew beyond the shadow of a doubt he was a new person. He had died down his old life and was willing to walk the straight and narrow with Hannah by his side if she let him.

"Afternoon Hannah," he said as she reached him.

"Mason, what brings you here?"

He smiled and took his hat off, "I wanted to come see you."

She smiled and tucked a lose strand of hair behind her ear, "Is that so?"

Even Hannah looked different now, it was as if this cloud of fog that kept skewed his outlook on life had been lifted, "Yes indeed, would you like to go for a walk with me?"

He saw her hesitate slightly but then she nodded, "Of course, I could use some fresh air before I have to go to the sisters meeting."

They walked in silence for a short while and as if they were both searching for words they spoke at the exact same time, "I wanted...." Mason started.

"What did you..." Hannah interrupted and then giggled.

"Well, it spent some time thinking about what you said."

Bending down he picked a small yellow flower and then handed it to her, "I have decided to stay here in Lancaster. My father was willing to baptize me so I'm once again part of the community."

The look on her face was priceless, and the way her eyes lit up made him want to kiss her there and then, but he refused to ruin a perfect moment.

"You did?" she asked breathlessly.

"Yes, you see, I left here thinking that the world was what I needed, and for some time it was fun, but after I returned here and saw you again, I realized what a big mistake that was."

He could tell she didn't know what to say by the way her mouth fell opened and closed, so he continued, "Hannah, I know a lot has happened and you're afraid of commitment, but I've always loved you and I want to spend the rest of my life proving that to you."

"Mason..." she started and looked down at the flower in her hand, "what if you decide to leave again?"

"I won't, my life is here now, my family and friends, and I want to be where you are." He stepped closer and cupped the side of her face, "Only if that is what you want."

Hannah leaned into his touch and a single tear ran down the side of her cheek which he wiped with the pad of his thumb.

"Do you promise to stay?" she asked in a trembling voice.

"I promise."

"Good because my heart would never survive if you broke it a second time," she said and walked into his arms.

"I'll protect it with my life."

****

Four months later, Hannah and Mason finally got married. Mason had laid down his former life and found his own feet amongst his fellow

Amish folk, but he would never have been able to do this without Hannah. She was his beacon in his dark night.

AMISH GROVE

HARRIET MARKS

68

Chapter I

Rain decorated the grassy fields of Lancaster County. The sky was a cloud grey, the sun remaining absent as the county mourned for the loss of William Bradshire, a carpenter that had been known throughout the county for his kindness and love towards the people around him.

Friends and family had gathered in the county's cemetery for William's funeral, one of the mourners being William's love, Mary Lee Warner. Out of everyone there, Mary was the most damaged from it. William's parents had passed on early in his life due to illnesses and the remaining family he had weren't as close. If anything, Mary was the only one there who truly was family to him.

As Bishop David spoke about his memories with William, Mary thought to herself how God could do such a thing, to take away an innocent being this early in his life. William was only in his mid-twenties, like Mary. He had so much to experience in his life, but it was stripped away from him so early due to the accident.

"If anyone has anything to say, speak now." Bishop David said, stepping back and letting anyone step forward to speak.

There was a long pause, silence being present as Mary thought to herself. Eventually, she took a step forward, standing in front of the casket as she let out a depressed sigh.

"William...had a beautiful soul," Mary said quietly, holding onto a wildflower, "a soul that I have yet to find in any other human being."

Everyone was watching her speak, seeing what Mary had in her hand and what she had to say about William being gone.

"I can't imagine not meeting him in my life...all the memories we've made together...all the laughter, the love...I'm going to miss it." Mary spoke as tears ran down her cheeks. "I don't know if I will find another William in my life."

Some of William's family members began to have tears fall too as they listened to Mary's words about their lost kin. Mary soon stepped back from the casket, having finished speaking on the behalf of William's death. Bishop David soon stepped forward again, wiping some tears from his own eyes.

"Thank you Mary...I will say, before I close in prayer, that it will be difficult to find another William in our lives." Bishop David said to Mary before opening his Bible.

Verses from the Bible were soon spoken out loud, everybody bowing their heads in prayer as Bishop David spoke. While everyone listened, Mary wasn't listening to the verses, in fact, she was in her own mind at this point.

"Why God...why would you take William away from me?" Mary thought to herself. "William didn't even get half way into his life...why would you take him now?"

As she struggled with the idea of William passing on, Bishop David finished reading the verses, quietly speaking the word amen as he closed his Bible, everybody soon leaving the scene of the funeral, letting the casket to be lowered into the grave. While the casket lowered, Mary was the only one present, witnessing her love's final presence on the surface of Earth.

In regards to funeral traditions of the Amish, flowers were not placed on the casket. For Mary though, traditions meant nothing to her in this occasion. She took the wildflower that she was holding in her hand and tossed it down into the undug grave, letting it land on the coffin before the gravediggers began to bury the coffin.

"I love you so much William." Mary said as the coffin soon disappeared from the soil piling on top. Tears continued to fall onto the soil as she left the site of the funeral.

Chapter II

Several years later...the county had returned back to its normal ways, except for Mary. Ever since William passed away, Mary wasn't her old self. Her old cheerful personality had passed on as well, leaving her a closed up, emotionless woman in her mid-twenties.

She tried to return back to a normal life by going to church, seeing if God might be able to help her find peace, but the more she went the church, the more she began to question God. At times, she would find herself being angry at God for taking William away this early in his life. Eventually, Mary stopped going to church, which brought the concern of Bishop David, leading him to go to Mary's home.

Her house was a little way from town, being near one of the farms. She lived in a large house that belonged to William and his parents. Now that William passed on, Mary now owned the house and lived in it by herself.

Bishop David knocked on the front door, waiting for it to be opened. It took a few knocks before the door finally opened, Mary standing there in a stone grey dress.

"Yes?" Mary quietly said, looking at him with her expressionless face.

"May I come in?" Bishop David asked softly, his expression being hopeful that she would accept his request.

Mary let out a quiet sigh before she nodded, stepping out of the way for Bishop David to come in.

"Thank you...Mary." He said, soon walking into her home, looking around.

Mary shut the door behind Bishop David, walking past him and sitting down on a chair in the living room, continuing what she was doing before he knocked. When Bishop David sat down across from her, he noticed that she was knitting a quilt.

"Oh...I see that you've been busy with making a quilt." Bishop David said, giving Mary a gentle smile.

"Quilts. I've been busy making quilts." She said quickly, pointing in the corner to a basket of several quilts.

Bishop David was surprised by the amount of quilts she had made. "That's quite the number of quilts Mary." He said with a small laugh after.

Mary raised her eyebrows as she continued to knit the quilt. "I've found that work is one of the few things that keeps me from thinking about the past." She said softly, not making eye contact with Bishop David.

"Oh...well...if that's what helps you find peace." He said quietly, rubbing the back of his neck before he finally decided to talk about why he wanted to talk to her. "Mary...I'm worried about you."

She heard Bishop David, stopping for a second before she continued knitting the quilt. "Why?" Mary questioned him.

"I'm concerned for you because you haven't been going to church for months." Bishop David finally said, looking at her with a worried expression. "You were always an avid church-goer when William..." He said before realizing what he said, stopping in mid-sentence.

Mary immediately looked up when Bishop David brought up William, her knitting ceasing before she let out a sigh of disbelief escape her lips. She set the quilt and knitting needle down. "Please, do not ever bring up William to me again when comparing me to then and now." Mary said, her voice trembling as she had grown an upset expression.

Bishop David had become silent as he listened to Mary finally speak to him.

"I'm no longer the Mary from then because of the events that happened, and if you want to visit me and tell me how I use to love church and that you're concerned with me not being there on Sundays, then don't even speak, you're wasting your breath." Mary said to him, her eyes staring into his intensely.

Bishop David heard everything she was saying before he let out a sigh of sympathy. "I'm sorry Mary that you're like this...I didn't come here today to chastise you about not attending church. I came here because I'm really concerned for what you've become. I want happiness for you, I want you to have that cheerful personality that everybody knew you for." He said softly, standing up from sitting, looking down at her. "Always remember Mary, we all face events in life that we don't want, but it's all a part of God's plan for something greater."

Mary just glared at him the whole time he spoke, not even acknowledging the things he said. "I would like you to leave."

Bishop David heard her request and nodded softly, walking away from where they were at and leaving the house.

She had watched him leave through the windows before she finally reached for her knitting needles and quilt, continuing to knit as she thought about what he said about God having a plan for everyone. To her, God's plan was killing William and taking away something that she loved most in the world, when she didn't have anyone else.

"Forget God." Mary said to herself quietly, having completely lost faith and love in God.

Chapter III

One stormy night soon had arrived in Lancaster County. Rain had arrived over the town and fields, the sound of sharp pellets hitting the roofs and windows of each building. The window whirled between each building, the sounds of wind wailing could be heard by anyone who was awake.

While the storm stayed present in the county, Mary was asleep in her bed, although she wasn't sleeping soundly. The red-headed woman was having a nightmare, causing her to toss back and forth in her sleep before some sort of sound interrupted her slumber.

KNOCK KNOCK KNOCK

Mary sat right up from her bed like a vampire in a coffin, rubbing her eyes. "What on Earth?" She said to herself, looking around the room as she wondered what caused her to wake up.

KNOCK KNOCK KNOCK

This time, the red-head heard the solution to the noise. "Who could be at my door in the middle of the night?" Mary got out of her bed, wrapping her blanket around herself to cover her nightgown. She made her way down the stairs of her home before seeing the front door. Once she got to the door, she slowly opened it, seeing who it was.

There was a man, about her age, with a young daughter about six-years-old. They were wet from head to toe, shivering as they looked at Mary.

"Please...do you have room in your home for my child and I? We come from far away to Lancaster County...we have no home, no food." The man said, his tone being a desperate one.

Mary had no idea that this was what waited for her on the other side of the door. "I...Well..." She looked at the two before she finally nodded quickly, stepping out of the way.

"Oh thank you...thank you!" The man said happily and emotionally. He quickly moved inside, Mary shutting the door behind the two. Even though they were inside, away from the rain, they still were shivering in the dark home. Mary saw how cold they were and immediately knew what they needed.

She quickly went over to the fireplace in the living room, taking two logs that were on the side of the hearth in a pile and putting them inside the fireplace. After a few attempts of trying to get a fire started, she eventually managed to do so, an orange glow illuminating the living room.

Once the man saw the fire, he moved his daughter close to the fireplace, trying to get her as warm as possible. Mary saw what he was trying to do and quickly went over to the eight-year-old, wrapping her blanket around the child. The man soon began to dry off her daughter while at the same time trying to get her warm.

"There you go...nice and warm now. Away from the cold rain." He said quietly to his daughter, holding her close as he sat in front of the fireplace with her.

The daughter shivered still, but the warmth from the fire and the blanket caused the shivering to decrease as the time went by.

Mary stood behind the two, watching them and making sure that they were okay. "Are you warm enough?" She asked them, having held one of the quilts she had made in her hands to give to the man.

"Yes...thank you kind miss." He said quietly, holding his daughter close before taking the quilt from Mary, wrapping it around himself.

With the two warming themselves up from the fire, Mary decided to grab another quilt for herself before sitting down on her couch. She wrapped the quilt around her body so she could be warm too. Since she now had two "guests" in her home, she didn't want to go upstairs, back to bed, with the knowledge that two strangers were downstairs in her home, two people who she had no idea who they were.

"Maybe they're thieves," Mary thought to herself, studying the two strangers. "Although...she looks pretty young to be a thief." She finally decided to speak up, wanting to figure out who they were. "Where did you two come from?"

The man looked back at her, hearing her question before he began to reply to her. "We came from Somerset County." The man answered, still trying to warm up his daughter.

"Oh...that's far from here." Mary replied, sitting down on her couch, looking at the man.

"It very much is..." The man nodded, looking at her. "Do you know if there's any housing here in Lancaster County?"

Mary heard her question before she shrugged. "I'm not too sure. Are you looking for a place to stay?"

The man nodded, looking down at his daughter. She had fallen into slumber and had a warm expression on her face and had stopped shivering, indicating she was no longer freezing. "Yes."

She heard him and asked some more questions in order to get to know him. "Why Lancaster County? I'm sure there's plenty of other settlements along the way."

"I just," The man began to say, rubbing the back of his neck nervously, "I don't know...I guess I've heard a lot of great things about Lancaster. Figured that it would be a great place for my daughter to grow up in."

Mary nodded when he stated that it'd be a good place for his daughter to grow up in. "Lancaster really is a nice place to grow up in...a good place to start a fam-" she began to say before stopping when she was about to say "family." It reminded her of what she has always wanted to have and that made her think of William and her. "Well, it's a good place to meet nice and caring people."

The man saw her reaction when she was talking about family, but decided not to question it in order to remain polite. "That's good to hear...by the way," the man began to say, looking at her once again, "what is your name?"

She heard him and replied softly. "Mary...my name is Mary Lee Warner."

When the man heard her, he smiled softly. "That's a beautiful name."

Mary smiled softly when he complimented her name. "What about you? What's your name?"

"Robert." He said quietly, before looking down at his daughter, gently stroking her hair. "The little one is Miriam."

Chapter IV

The next morning had arrived, the rain was now gone, the only trace of rain being the puddles in the dirt. Mary decided to help Robert and Miriam out by going down to the church to see Bishop David could help them out.

Entering the church, there were only a few people present in the pews, praying to the Lord about whatever comes to their attention. Bishop David was not preaching, considering it was a Tuesday, so chances were he was at his home.

"Doesn't look like he's here." Mary said, turning around and leading Robert and Miriam out.

"Who are we looking for exactly?" Robert said, holding his daughter's hand as they walked towards Bishop David's house.

"We're looking for David, Lancaster County's bishop. He might be able to help you out with moving here." Mary replied, reaching the bishop's house before knocking on the door. Not too long after the knock, the door opened, Bishop David standing there.

"Mary?" He said, a little surprised. "What brings you here today?"

Mary explained the whole story to him, telling the bishop that Robert and Miriam showed up in the middle of the night, needing a place to stay and that they wanted to move to Lancaster.

"I see..." Bishop David said quietly, scratching his beard as he thought about it. "Unfortunately, there isn't any houses available right now."

Mary heard the news and let out a quiet groan. "So where will they stay if they don't have a home?"

Bishop David heard her before looking at the two, looking at Mary again. "Can I talk to you privately Mary?"

Mary was confused as to why, but nodded as she stepped inside the bishop's house. "What did you want to talk to me about?"

Bishop David looked at her before he let out a quiet sigh. "I wanted to talk to you privately about where they're going to stay. I believe they should continue living at your house until a new house can be built here in the county."

She listened to what he said before hearing his statement about the two staying at her home. "What? No. I can't have people living at my house."

Bishop David gave her a confused look. "Why not? You have one of the biggest houses here in Lancaster County. You're not living with anyone. There's plenty of room in the house for someone."

"Because, I don't have enough food to feed two more people. I don't want to start housing people." Mary was quick to say, folding her arms. "I can't let strangers come into my home and make themselves acquainted to the hou-"

"Mary." Bishop David interrupted, clearly showing he was getting irritated with her. "Enough with the excuses. I'm not going to force you to let them in. I'm only suggesting you give the two of them a home. It's not permanent, but where else are they going to go?" He asked Mary, looking at her with a serious expression. "They can't move into anyone else's home. They all have families, rather large ones too."

She listened to him, looking into his eyes as she thought about everything he was saying. Bishop David was right in many ways. Most families in the county had large families, homes that were already crowded. With Mary's house, it was just her. He even said that it wasn't permanent, so it'd be something that Mary didn't have to deal with for too long.

"I guess...I could have them stay for a little while." Mary finally admitted, realizing that she could be a little generous.

"Thank you Mary." Bishop David said before leading her back outside, now facing Robert. "We will discuss adding a house whenever I meet my colleagues. Until we can get a house added to the county, you'll have to stay with Mary for the time being."

Robert listened to what Bishop David said, nodding softly. "Okay, thank you."

Bishop David smiled softly, heading back into the house before closing the door.

Robert and Miriam turned toward Mary, looking at her. "So...are we going to back to the nice lady's house?" Miriam asked her father.

Mary heard her and couldn't help but smile. "Yes...yes you are."

Robert watched the two interact before he couldn't help but smile, seeing this stranger being so nice to his daughter.

"Alright. Let's head back to the house so I can get a room prepped up for you two." Mary said, clapping her hands together when she knew what she needed to do.

Chapter V

A couple of months passed by in Mary's household. The two strangers that had showed up on her doorstep were now friends of hers, having brightened up the household little by little. As Mary got to know Robert, he started feeling more and more comfortable around him, the two even joking around with each other.

With Miriam, she started to look up towards Mary as a mother figure, every now and then the little girl called Mary mom. Mary would hear this and laugh, finding it humorous that Robert's daughter called her mom.

While everyone was getting along just fine, Mary started to remember William again, every time she looked at Robert. There was something about Robert that reminded her of William. It might've been the way he made her laugh or the way he showed kindness to people. Whatever it was, Mary could see William through Robert, which made her think about if she found another William in her life.

It was now 6 PM and Robert and Miriam had finished eating dinner with Mary. When they finished, Robert decided to take Miriam to bed, since she started dozing off during dinner. Once she was in bed, she was out cold.

"She must've been really tired today. Miriam never goes to bed this early." Robert said, walking back into the kitchen. "I don't blame her...she didn't sleep that well last night."

"Oh poor thing." Mary said, cleaning the dishes in the sink. "I hope she rests well tonight."

"She probably will." Robert said, walking over before leaning against the counter. "So...what do you want to do?"

Mary continued to wash the dishes before she stopped, soon looking at him. "What do you mean?"

"Well I mean...Miriam is in bed early. Do you want to go out for a walk?" Robert replied, looking at her and waiting to hear an answer.

She looked at him before looking down at the dishes, thinking about his offer before setting the plates down. "I would enjoy that."

He smiled brightly before he walked out of the kitchen, planning on getting his jacket.

It didn't take long before the two were on an adventure, walking around the county in the early evening. The sky was an vibrant orange, the sun easing itself behind the hills.

"Wow...that's a beautiful sunset." Robert said softly, looking at it.

"It sure is." Mary said quietly, looking at it before she looked at Robert. With the two of them having grown closer, she soon started to think more in regards of making their relationship a bit more than friends. "Can I show you something?"

Robert heard her, turning his head and looking at her before he smiled softly. "Yeah of course."

Mary smiled brightly before leading him into the woods, walking in a certain direction. As for Robert, he wasn't sure where she was taking him, which made him a little nervous. Eventually, the two arrived in a rather large open area in the woods, a grass area that was decorated with wildflowers.

"Wow..." Robert quietly said to himself, stepping forward and starting to walk towards the flowers. "They're beautiful."

Mary stood behind Robert, watching his response before walking with him again. "I know. I love coming to this place. It reminds me of so many happy memories." She said before she began to lay down in the grass, looking at the sky that had become as orange as a Doris Longwing Butterfly's wing.

Robert watched what she did before he followed her actions, lying next to her as the two watched the sky. "You have quite the spot...especially one that you value." He smiled softly, relaxing on the grass.

The two watched the sky for a few, enjoying the time to relax with each other. Eventually, Robert spoke up, a question that had been resonating within him.

"How come you didn't want to let us live with you a few months ago?" He quietly said, still looking at the sky, some clouds gently moving along in the sky.

Mary heard him and gave him a confused look. "What do you mean?"

"You were talking to Bishop David the morning after the rainstorm. You told him that you didn't want anyone staying at the house because you didn't have enough food and didn't want housing people. Part of me though doesn't believe that."

Mary listened to what Robert was saying, her expression staying confused before her expression became more of a look of hesitant.

"There's something more than not enough food and not wanting to house people huh? You don't have to tell me, but just know I'm here if you want to talk." Robert said quietly, wanting to assure that she could trust him.

She listened to what he said before she began biting her own lip, thinking to herself before she let out a quiet sigh. "There is...there's a lot more to it. I think it's fair that you should know."

He heard her response to his question and turned onto his side, looking at her now as she began to speak about what the reason for not wanting anyone to live with her.

"It all has to do with a man I loved...a man named William." Mary said quietly.

Chapter VI

William Bradshire...a carpenter of Lancaster County. Most of the county knew him as the kind man who cared about everyone around him, even the ones who didn't care for him. William was the prime example of what it means to follow Christ's footsteps. He showed a strong love towards God, helped out around his community, showed love towards everyone, taught the youth about the Bible, and that's just the peak of the iceberg.

Sometimes in life though, bad things can occur that change one's life. For William, it was losing his parents at the age of eighteen. With his parents gone, he now owned the house, but that meant nothing to William. For a long time, he had struggled with the fact that his parents were gone, but during this time, he still continued to help people, having put them first before himself.

A great example of William putting others first was one cold, dark night. There was a knock on his door, the knock having echoed the entire silent household. When William opened his front door, he found a shivering girl his age, looking up at him. This girl was Mary.

The young girl had ran away from home, angry at her parents and her peers around her community. She was looking for a place to stay, which was she ended up on William's doorstep, a stranger to him. William was caring enough to immediately let her in; he even allowed her to stay as long as she needed. Even though she could've left any time, she found herself a priceless friendship.

Eventually, as time progressed, the redhead soon fell in love with William, the same happening with the boy. The two ended up revealing their love for each other when they discovered and rested in the grass area in the woods with the wildflowers. Ever since then, they were two peas in a pod.

As time progressed, they became closer and closer, almost being one soul. Mary began helping out in the community with him while developing a strong love of God since William introduced her to Him. Eventually, William decided that he was going to ask Mary for her hand in marriage, but his colleagues asked for his help in finishing the construction of a barn.

Unfortunately, William never had the chance to pop the question due to the accident. While he was watching his colleagues raise one of the barn walls up by pulling it up with ropes, the ropes snapped and the wall soon fell on William, his chances of escaping the wall very low with how fast the whole situation took. Sadly, William didn't survive the heavy barn wall crushing him.

Word soon got out around the county about William dying from the accident, which Mary soon heard about. She was devastated, crushed, her heart torn into pieces for the loss of her one true love.

After William had passed, Mary was given the house, considering she basically lived there and was a member of the community. During this time, Mary closed herself off from the rest of the world, locking herself away in her home, mourning the loss of William. She even decided to not let anyone into the house after the loss in order to keep the house peaceful, like it was when William and her were in it.

Even in the present, Mary still has nightmares about the whole incident, nightmares that remind her of the loss of William.

"If only I were there to stop him...to get him out of the way...If only I were there...he'd still be alive."

Chapter VII

Once Mary finished telling Robert the story, she had developed some tears from the memory of William's death.

"Now you know why I don't let anyone into the house...I know...it sounds insane, for the girlfriend of someone who has departed to keep the house like a temple. You must think I'm crazy..." Mary said quietly, wiping her tears.

"Oh no..." Robert said, looking at her. "I don't think you're insane at all...I can see why you value the house so much. All the memories with William...the laughter...the peace...everything about it...you don't want anyone to ruin this place for you." He said softly, gently resting his hand on hers. "I'm sorry...I didn't know this was the reason why you didn't want us here."

Mary heard him and finally broke down, tears rolling down her cheeks as she covered her face with her hands, muffled crying heard behind it. Robert reached for her and wrapped his arms around her, holding her close as he embraced her.

"Shhh...it's okay...Mary." Robert quietly said, stroking her hair gently to calm her down. "It's okay..."

After years of suppressing the memories of William and her, the pain she has endured from remembering his death, the many tears she had held back, she finally broke down and let her tears flow.

"I miss him so much...every day I wish I could see him again...tell him that I wish I could've saved him from the wall...I wish I could've done something." She said, pressing her face against Robert's shoulder as she shook from her crying.

"You couldn't do anything Mary...you had no idea that would happen..." Robert said softly, continuing to hold her close as she cried against him. "Look on the bright side...with William having a strong love for God, he's finally in Heaven where he can be with God...walk along with him...talk to him...laugh with him."

With Robert's words entering Mary's ears, it made her cry more. He was right in the sense that she wouldn't have known and that he's in a better place now. Her heart ached as she recalled all the memories of William from when they met to his death. All the memories were mainly happy and ones that would make her laugh whenever she looked back to them. Even though William was gone, she remembered one thing...William lives on through her. The memories, the house, the ideology, everything that William was made up of lives on through Mary. With this thought, she felt like she could finally get over the tragedy of losing William and achieve peace.

"Thank you...Robert...Thank you." Mary said quietly, looking up at him with tears in her eyes.

Robert looked down at her, confused as to why she was telling him thank you. "For what?" He laughed gently, wiping the tears away from her eyes.

"For saying all of those things about William and I...I've spent all these years holding onto William's tragedy and blaming myself for not being able to help him, but now I can finally find peace and let go of the tragedy...thank you...Robert." She finally said, looking at him as she gently reached up, stroking his cheek before she finally decided to lean in, kissing him gently.

Robert was caught off guard with the kiss, his eyebrows raising as she held her in his arms. Eventually, she broke the kiss, resting her head on his should. "Let's go back home...it's getting late." Mary said quietly, her eyes now closed.

Even though Robert had thought about pushing their relationship to another level, there was something that was holding him from reaching that level, something that had followed him from his previous home.

Chapter VIII

Many weeks had passed by since Mary told Robert about her past. Mary was in a much brighter mood, slowly building herself up again by socializing with people, going to church again, which made Bishop David happy, and she started wearing colorful clothes again.

Robert was thinking about what Mary had done in the wildflower area in the woods on the porch. He wanted to moved towards the next step, but the past was catching up with him.

"Hey!" Mary called out, coming up to the house with Miriam. "We've got dinner!"

He snapped back into reality, smiling gently when he saw the two. "Oh...that's wonderful. Looks delicious." Robert said, standing up and helping them take the food inside the house.

"I decided to cook something special for you...to thank you for helping me return back to my old self again."

Robert smiled and chuckled nervously, rubbing the back of his neck. "Oh...you don't have to do that."

"But papa," Miriam spoke out, looking at him, "look at the food! It looks delicious! At least let mom...Mary cook it for me."

Both Robert and Mary laughed at Miriam's comment, Mary picking her up and holding her.

"Okay, well if Robert doesn't want his special dinner, then I'll cook it for you." She said, walking in with the child.

"That'd be fantastic!" Miriam exclaimed happily.

Robert followed behind the two with the groceries, his expression being lost in thought as he thought about the past.

Dinner time soon arrived, everyone now seated at the table as they waited for Mary to come in with the special dinner.

"Whatever she's cooking, it smells delicious." Miriam said, excited to eat.

In a matter of minutes, Mary came out with a cooked turkey, the skin being a golden crisp.

Even though Robert wasn't asking for a special dinner, he was impressed with how the turkey came out. "Wow, looks really good Mary."

She smiled brightly, setting the plate down. "Well I'm glad you like it so much. I've got more coming out. I cooked some corn, made so mashed potatoes, have some greens." Mary explained to them as she walked back into the kitchen.

It took a few trips for her before she finally could sit down at the table with the two. "Alright, dig in." Mary said, taking her knife and fork, cutting into the turkey and scooping up a little bit of everything.

The dinner that they had all together was nice. Lots of laughter, lots of compliments, complete joy filled the room between Miriam and Mary, although Robert was most of the time quiet. After dinner, Miriam decided to go play with her doll in the living room while Mary and Robert were in the kitchen, cleaning the dishes.

While they were in there, Robert remained quiet, lost in his thoughts as he kept trying to shake it off. It didn't take too long though for Mary to see something was bothering him.

"You've been awfully quiet this evening...is there something wrong?" Mary asked him, continuing to wash the dishes.

"No." Robert said vaguely, not wanting to get into what was bothering him.

"You sure?" She said softly, looking at him. "You seem like you're thinking really hard about something."

"Don't worry about it." Robert said to her, trying to avoid explaining his thoughts.

Eventually, Mary let out a quiet sigh before setting her dish down, turning toward Robert.

"You know if something is troubling you, you can te-" Mary began to say to him.

"Drop it." Robert said harshly, looking at her for a few quick seconds before he finally set his plate down, shaking his head. "Just forget it...I'm going to bed." He said, leaving the kitchen and walking upstairs.

Mary was shocked by the way Robert reacted, considering it wasn't normal for Robert to be this way.

Miriam heard the commotion from the living room, looking at Mary. "Is papa upset about something?" She said with a concerned voice.

Mary heard Miriam and shook her head. "Don't worry about it dear. He just needs some time to himself."

Chapter IX

Robert currently laid in Mary's bed upstairs, his eyes closed as he tried sleeping. He didn't mean to snap at Mary, but considering his thoughts were getting to him, it was bound to happen. As he attempted to sleep, he soon felt something lay next to him, which interrupted his slumber. He opened his eyes and turned to look and see if it was Mary.

Of course, he was right in this situation. Mary was in her nightgown, having crawled in bed with Robert, getting cozy. Once he saw it was Mary, he returned back to his previous position, his back facing her. Still trying to avoid breaking the news to Mary, he soon felt her arms around his stomach, her body soon pressing against his back.

"What's going on with you? You're usually not like this." She said softly, resting her head against his back.

"I don't know Mary...I don't know." Robert said quietly, his eyes still closed.

"I feel like you do know Robert." Mary finally said. "I just feel like you don't want to tell me what you're thinking of."

He heard what she said, but didn't reply to it. The only thing he did was sit in silence with his eyes closed, trying to fall into slumber.

"You know I'm here if you want to tell me what's bothering you. I think it'd be healthy if you did though because you won't get any sleep with you thinking about whatever you're thinking. I know from experience." Mary quietly said, now closing her eyes as she rested her head against his back.

Robert listened to what she was saying before he let out a quiet sigh, trying to think about how he would explain his thoughts to her. Eventually, he decided to be straightforward with her.

"You know why I decided to move to Lancaster County?" He asked Mary quietly.

She merely shook her head against his back, indicating that she didn't know why he moved here. "Aside from finding a new home, no I don't."

Robert listened to what she had to say before he continued. "I left my previous home because my wife walked out on Miriam and I."

When Mary heard this, her eyes opened up and she sat up, looking down at him. "What? That's horrible! Why would she do that?"

Once Mary sat up, Robert turned so that he was laying on his back, now looking up at her. "To be honest...maybe I married the wrong person. She just...everything seemed fine to me. She was a good mother, I was a good father, we lived a happy life, but then one day..." He said before stopping, thinking back to that day before telling Mary what happened.

"Sara?" He called out, looking around his home. "Where are you?

While he walked around the house, Miriam watched him, not understanding what was going on. "Papa? What's going on?"

"I can't find mom. She's gone." Robert said, his tone being a little more scared. "Maybe she left something saying where she went. Yeah...she leaves notes."

"Maybe...I'll help you try and find something" Miriam said, getting off of the couch before walking around their home, trying find anything that could lead to the mystery of where Robert's wife went.

Eventually, Miriam found a note that had fallen on the side of the bed. "Papa!" She called out. "I found a note!"

Robert immediately ran into the room, seeing the note in Miriam's hand. He took the note from her and began reading it. Although the hope he had on his expression when he found the note soon faded the more he continued to read it. In fact, he soon had become emotionless from what was written on the note.

"What does it say papa?" Miriam asked, looking up at him.

Robert finished reading the note, looking down at Miriam before folding the note in half, tucking it into his pocket. "Don't worry about it sweetheart. I think though...we need to move away from this county."

When Miriam heard this, she was completely confused. "Why? Why do we need to move?"

He heard her before he picked her up, looking around the house one last time. "Because I think we will find somewhere else that'll be better for the both of us."

———————

"We basically left the county with nothing but the clothes on our back. I couldn't stand living in the same county as her and live in a house that we lived in together." Robert said quietly, looking at Mary as he finished explaining his story. "Would you stay in the same place if you found out your love left you and your child for someone else?"

When Mary heard this, she let out a depressed sigh. "No...I don't think I would." She said quietly. "Is that what's been on your mind today?"

Robert heard her before nodding softly. "I've been thinking about it for a long time now...I've wanted to move onto the next step in our relationship, but...I fear that something would happen again...I fear the odds of you walking out on us."

Once Robert said that, Mary spoke up in a more serious tone. "Robert...look at me."

Robert did as told and look into her eyes, seeing what she would say.

"I would never do that...ever in my life." Mary said, looking at him as she gently rested her hand on his cheek. "I wouldn't do something to hurt you and Miriam...I love you both, with all my heart." She said to him before she gently kissed him, breaking it soon after before resting her head on his chest. "You don't need to worry about me every walking out on you two...I care about you two so much that my heart aches. I wouldn't even think about walking out on you two."

When Robert heard this, he let out a relieved sigh, his arms wrapping around her and hugging her against him. "I love you so much Mary..."

"I love you too Robert..."

THE END

AMISH ANGELS

NANCY MANN

"Father, please don't –!"

The plea came too late and was unheeded as a bucket of cold water was released onto Emilia's head, about her bonnet and down along the front of her dress.

"Father!" she screamed, furiously. "Why on earth would you do such a thing!"

Jumping from her chair, she whirled around to face him, her brown eyes flashing with anger. To her dismay, he was beaming as if he had bestowed some act of kindness upon her.

"Emilia, it is summertime! You are cooped up within the walls of a house, knitting a sweater," he replied, reaching out to take her arm. "I do believe that the sunshine is calling your name."

"A sweater that is now ruined!" Emilia complained but allowed for Abel to lead her from the dark stone house into the yard, dripping water heavily along the way. Her two younger sisters were engaged in a game of hopscotch on the road, their long braids flailing in the wind.

"You see? Even the children know better than to stay indoors when the day is fraught with beauty. What kind of example are you setting for the young ones?"

"Father, I do not have time for trivial tasks. I needed to have that sweater finished for the marketplace. After which I have to begin making supper. Now I will be up half the night knitting!"

"Ah! One less sweater at the marketplace will not be the end of days. Also, you do not have to make supper tonight. We have been invited to the home of our neighbor." Emilia turned and looked at him suspiciously at the sudden announcement.

"Which neighbor?" she demanded. Again, Abel smiled, undaunted by his eldest daughter's scrutiny.

"The new members of our community. They reside only a few houses down the road."

"Father, you don't mean that sour faced man with the sullen little girl, do you? I did not like the looks of those two at church. They seem to not like being here. We don't know anything about them."

"My dear, you do not like the look of anyone. That is because you don't truly look at anyone. And that is why we are going this evening; to learn about them and make them feel welcome. "

"Oh father, that is simply not accurate. I do not engage in silliness like other women. I much prefer my own company to idle chit chat. There is no harm in that. I believe it shows that I have a strong head on my shoulders."

"Indeed, it does, my daughter. Once in a while, however, you can relax and enjoy the sunshine." Emilia did not reply. This was an old argument. Since the passing of her mother six years earlier, Abel Troyer had done his best to keep his three daughters in high spirits. The two youngest had eventually moved on from the unexpected death but Emilia had clung to the memory of her mother like a spider web shawl, refusing to let light into her life. Abel desperately missed the infectious sound of Emilia's laughter, a tone which used to ring through the hills of their community like a tinkling bell.

"Regardless, father, I see no reason why we should join Mr. Bawell and his daughter for supper," Emilia finally said. "But if you feel you must, by all means, do go without me."

"It is my wish that we attend supper at their residence and so we shall. I am still the head of this household, Emilia. I do not appreciate being contradicted." Abel was beginning to lose his good humor. He did not understand why everything had to be a fight with Emilia. When his wife had been alive, Emilia had been the model child, obedient and respectful. He knew she only wanted to be left alone to her brooding but he would not have it. She was perfectly healthy, a lovely, kind hearted woman who deserved happiness. It was his job as her father to ensure that she received it. Emilia wisely closed her mouth and turned to face her siblings as her father walked off into the back part of the yard, seeming to have no more interest in teasing his child.

"Emmy, will you play with us?" Collette called, her blonde hair almost white in the droplets of sunlight. Emilia forced herself to smile and shook her head. For a fleeting moment, she was tempted to join the children but she pushed the thought from her mind.

"Not today, Collette. I have work to do."

"You always have work to do, Emmy!" Evelyn pouted. Collette took her younger sister's hand and pulled the nine-year-old toward the veranda.

"She is busy taking care of us, Evie. We are going to mammi and dawdy's now anyway. We must get dressed."

"Wait one moment, Collette. You're going to mammi and dawdy's house? Father just said that we are going to our new neighbor's for supper. Are you certain?"

Collette paused at the door to allow Evelyn to pass.

"You and papa are going to Aaron Bawell's for supper. Evie and I are going to mammi and dawdy's." The girls disappeared into the house and Emilia was left on the porch, still dripping from her father's cold water bath. She narrowed her smoky eyes. Why is he sending Evie and Collette to our grandparents' house? What is papa up to? She cringed inwardly as she had her suspicions.

"Emilia, why do you insist on being so stubborn?"

"What is it, father? What have I done now?"

Abel sighed heavily and stared at his daughter as she descended the stairs from her bedroom.

"You know full well that you cannot attend this supper wearing working clothes. Please change into more appropriate attire." Emilia blinked her solemn eyes at him.

"But father, I believed this to be work." Abel scowled and pointed firmly up the staircase.

"You will do as I say immediately, Emilia. And that is quite enough of your impudence for one day." Emilia hung her head in shame, immediately reading her father's anger and slightly stung by his words. Abel was not one to raise his voice in anger.

"Yes father. I'm sorry." She hurried back up to change her clothes and wondered why she had performed such a defiant act. She knew that her father would not have allowed her to visit the Bawell house dressed in rags. It was disrespectful. Lately she had been feeling more and more feisty and if she was not already well into her late twenties, she would have thought that she was due to experience rumspringa. She had briefly experimented with cigarettes and beer when she was younger but she had since been baptized and was very happy in the community. Well, as happy as Emilia could be. There was an unsurmountable void which had filled Emilia since the death of her young mother. She was eternally grateful for the consistency and love given by Abel, however, Emilia and her mother had a bond that seemed to outlive death. Time did not heal her pain and eventually Emilia had succumbed to the fact that she was destined to be discontent for the remainder of her life. Yet lately, the sorrow had turned into some sort of boiling anger and no matter how Emilia tried, she could not seem to tame the beast which was growing within her.

Moments later, she was descending the stairs in a freshly ironed dark blue dress, a starch white bonnet covering her thick head of hair. Abel beamed happily.

"You look lovely. Much better. Shall we?" He offered his arm to his daughter and they started out the door.

"Father, why have you sent the children to mammi and dawdy's this evening?"

"Ah because this evening is for the older people, my dear daughter." Emilia swallowed a knowing grunt but said nothing. As they strolled up the walkway toward the Bawell household, the front door flew open and Emilia was facing the petulant stare of a six-year-old child. Her blue eyes looked like frosted panes of glass as she took in the sight of the two strangers on the porch.

"Good evening, Amity," Abel boomed amiably. "How are you this fine night?"

The girl did not respond and instead turned and disappeared out of view. Emilia gave her father a look but the older man did not meet her eyes. A moment later, Aaron Bawell appeared at the door.

"Please, come in," he said, extending the front door for them to enter. Abel smiled and nodding his thanks while Emilia reluctantly followed.

"May I introduce my daughter, Emilia?" Abel said, removing hat and gesturing toward Emilia.

"Yes," Aaron replied nodding and closing the door. Emilia was slightly taken aback by his disinterested response. In her grief, Emilia had not been interested in the prospect of marriage despite her father's endless prompting.

"It is not healthy for a woman to go through life without a companion, Emilia," Abel had told her countless times. "What of children?"

"I have two daughters in Evelyn and Collette," she had replied, only half jokingly. She had not the stomach to think of child bearing when her own mother had not had the chance to watch her daughters grow up. Eventually, Abel had forsaken the quest to marry off his oldest daughter. However, she had more callers than anyone else in her community and the reason for that was simple. She was the ideal wife. She was hard working, compassionate and a deep thinker. She possessed patience and everyone was a friend to her. Also, she was incredibly lovely, with long honey blonde hair and wide, innocent brown eyes, framed in long eyelashes. Whenever Emilia flashed an elusive smile, the entire world seemed to follow her lead. Even after years of rejecting suitor after suitor, they still came knocking on her door, eager to see her wed to them.

This is why Aaron Bawell's abrupt greeting was so stunning to Emilia. He was apparently unimpressed by Emilia's presence. He does not know you, Emilia reasoned, following the men into the sitting room. He has only been in our district for two weeks. He has no reason to give you a second look. Even as Emilia thought the words, she felt a strange pang of longing. She oddly wished him to look at her again. And again. You must stop thinking this way! She chided herself. Your thoughts are that of a child in puppy love! But Emilia could not stop staring at the newcomer and taking in all the details of his strong physique. His voice was deep and mellifluous and Emilia thought she could listen to him speak all day long. She felt a blush color her cheeks and she wondered what it was about Aaron which set him apart from the others who had bid for her hand in marriage. Certainly he was handsome but many men could claim the same. He donned a beard, an indication that he was married but there had been no mention of a mother for his young daughter. Emilia suddenly realized that she was very interested in learning more about the man in whose house she sat. Aaron and Abel were having a conversation of which Emilia heard none. As they finished speaking, Aaron looked about the room, somewhat confused.

"Amity!" Aaron called out. "Join us, please."

His demand was met with no response and sighing heavily after a moment, Aaron rose to his feet.

"Excuse me," he apologized before disappearing into the home. Emilia listened as his footsteps ascended up the staircase.

"Father, what on earth are we doing here?" Emilia asked, feeling distinctly uncomfortable. Abel gave her a sidelong look and smiled briefly.

"I believe you know what we are doing her, Emilia. Aaron Bawell is a successful carpenter. He is new to the community and has not been swayed by your endless rejection. He will be a perfect match for you."

"Father!" Emilia groaned. "I had hoped you had stopped with this matchmaking foolishness long ago."

"Emilia, it is not foolishness to want your children to be happy and begin a family. You are not going to be a young woman forever, child. You must consider your future."

"Father, I – "her words were cut short as Aaron returned to the sitting room, almost dragging along his daughter.

"Papa, I don't want them to be here," Amity Bawell snarled, glaring viciously at the strangers in her living room. Against the flickering kerosene lanterns, she almost looked diabolical, her small upper lip curled above her teeth, blue eyes aflame. She was otherwise a very pretty child, a spitting image of her father. She had long, straight black hair and cornflower blue eyes. Her features were softer, less defined than Aaron with his high cheekbones but she also had the extra fat of a small child.

"You will mind your manners!" Aaron snapped back, shooting an embarrassed look toward Abel.

"I do not like you!" Amity yelled, hands on her hips, addressing Emilia. Emilia was shocked by the defiance in the girl. She could not imagine either of her sisters ever speaking in such a way. I don't believe I am overly fond of you either, little devil, Emilia thought, narrowing her eyes at the child.

"Amity! You will stop this insolence immediately!" Aaron thundered, rising to his feet once more. "We are in the presence of guests. Your mother would be ashamed of your behavior!"

As if her father had physically struck her, Amity seemed to crumble to the floor. Her face went waxen and her eyes filled with tears. The deviousness evaporated and suddenly Emilia was staring at an ashen faced child. For a moment, she felt her heart crack. She had never seen a sorrier sight. Amity opened her mouth as if she were about to speak but no words fluttered from her small, pink lips. Then, tears streaked her chubby face and she ran, sobbing, from the room. Heavily,

Aaron reclaimed his seat beside Abel. There was an awkward silence as everyone searched for the right words to speak. Finally, Abel cleared his throat, standing.

"We will call another time, Aaron," Emilia's father said magnanimously, ushering Emilia to her feet. "Young girls can have their bad days. I understand. I have three of them."

Abel put a smile to his statement to ease the younger man's discomfort but Aaron looked devastated, his deep blue eyes troubled and full.

"Every day is a bad day." He seemed to have heard the way his words sounded and he quickly rose to his feet.

"I apologize. I thought we had been here long enough for her to accept visitors. This transition has been extremely difficult on Amity." Aaron looked imploringly at Abel for understanding, completely ignoring Emilia. Inwardly she was shaking her head. You are far too soft on the child. You should not make excuses, Emilia thought. These people are not the right fit for this community. We do not rear our children to act so recklessly.

"Of course it has! She is but a small girl. She cannot be expected to understand so much change in so little time," Abel assured him. "Give her time."

"I will speak to the Bishop about her," Aaron promised, ushering them toward the door. "Once more, please forgive this disruption. I will reschedule our meal for another time."

"Please, do not worry. Perhaps next time you will visit with us. Evelyn is only a few years older than Amity. A friend may do her a world of good." Aaron looked thoughtful at the suggestion and nodded. The men bid each other adieu and Aaron closed the door in their wake without so much as a glance at Emilia. Again, she was stunned by his rudeness. Abel took Emilia's arm and guided her down the path leading to their modest house moments down the road. When she was quite sure they were out of earshot, Emilia turned to her father.

"Lord above, I have never seen such an ill behaved child in all of my life!" she exploded. "And that man, he's rude – "

"Emilia – "Abel attempted to cut her off but she was not finished.

"He barely spoke one full word to me. I see that the apple does not fall far from the tree! Can you imagine raising a child so willful – "

"Emilia – "

"And you, you father, why on God's green earth would you ever consider him a match for me?"

"Are you quite finished with your diatribe?" Abel asked tiredly, releasing her arm as they approached their house.

"You can't say that you weren't shocked at her behavior, father," Emilia said, baffled by his calm demeanor.

"I was not," Abel replied. Emilia arched an eyebrow, her brown eyes cynical.

"How not?"

"I was not surprised because you and your sisters behaved very similarly after your mother passed also." A wave of dizziness overwhelmed Emilia as his words set in, instantly followed by deep regret.

"You mean to tell me that Amity's mother has recently passed away?" she whispered.

"Yes. Not three weeks ago. That is why Aaron has uprooted his life and started fresh here. Amity could not bear to be in their home without her mother. He is doing his best for his daughter. You could stand to be more empathetic, daughter. You know better than anyone how difficult a time this is for someone in their position."

Emilia paused on the veranda, staring after her father. Slowly, she turned to stare up into the dusky sky. Her heart was heavy with sadness but for the first time since she could remember, the woe she felt was not for herself but for the small girl missing her mother and the man who could not take her pain away.

II

The following morning, Emilia dressed and fed her sisters before delivering them to their school. Their morning chatter was often the highlight of Emilia's day but that dawn, she could not get the sight of Amity Bawell's anguished blue eyes out of her head as if they were etched into her skull. Oh how she understood the poor child's misery and she desperately wished that there was a way to help the girl overcome her fresh loss. Of course, she knew from personal experience that there was no such way. The Bishop would tell her that time, family and community would help expel the pain but Emilia knew that was a lie he would tell everyone. Over and above that, Emilia found her mind traveling to Aaron's Bawell. He was still such a young man to be widowed. Abel had informed her that they had been wed eight years when cancer claimed Aaron's wife, Beth. She had been sickly for a very long while before finally succumbing to her grave. Amity had watched her mother wither away before her eyes and when she finally did go to her final rest, Aaron had immediately acted, taking Amity away from the horrible memories and the house in which her mother had suffered so greatly.

"No child should ever have to see their parent in a state like that," Able had said sadly. "Especially one so young. They cannot begin to reconcile what is happening. In a way, it is a blessing that your mother was take so quickly. She was never in agony which you girls had to witness."

Emilia swallowed the lump in her throat and nodded but she wasn't sure if she agreed. Maybe mama wasn't in agony but we were. And some of us still are. Emilia forced herself to think about Aaron and Amity. She vowed that she would befriend the newcomers at once. It would not make their life more bearable but it would help shoulder the burden they were carrying. The Bishop had been right about one thing; community and family did assist the process somewhat.

After sending the children off and promising to pick them up that afternoon, Emilia carefully constructed a basket of wicker and filled it with several thought-filled items. There was a freshly knit blanket she had intended to sell at the market, jars of preserves and honey, a mutton pie and a bouquet of wildflowers. She gently wrapped the basket in another wool blanket and carried the package outside and down the laneway. There was a charged nervousness about her as she knocked on the door to the Bawell house. There was no sign of movement from within the walls but the curtains were drawn. Emilia knocked again but to her disappointment, there was no response. *Ah, well I imagine Amity is in school and Aaron is off at work although Lord knows they should be home in their grief. I will just leave this here. I did not pen a note. Maybe I will run home, write a note and bring it back.* Emilia set the gift down on the small porch and was on her way to retrieve a pen and paper. Suddenly, one of the straps to her bonnet came loose and just before a short wind carried it off, Emilia reached up and snatched it back, her whole body turning. Lowering herself from the balls of her feet, she realized she was facing the Bawell house again. Aaron Bawell was standing at the door, staring at her strangely. He was wearing only a white cotton undershirt and a pair of trousers, his beard unkempt and his feet were bare. Even so, he looked incredibly handsome, his black hair a disheveled mess about his finely lined face. He looked down at the basket on the porch and then back to Emilia. She offered him a timid smile.

"My family sent you some goods to help you along," she called out. Again, his steely blue eyes looked at the package. Without a word, he turned and slammed the door behind him, leaving the present on the dusty deck.

"You must not be offended, daughter. He is grieving," Abel told Emilia when she reiterated what happened.

"I know he is grieving, father but even you have to admit that it was unfathomably rude!" Abel shrugged nonchalantly and took a sip of his tea.

"You must not forsake them in their time of need, Emilia. People often are the most trying during their darkest hour of need. It is God's way of testing you to see if you are capable of maintain humility and patience. Also, Aaron has agreed to come here for supper tomorrow evening." Emilia dropped her parring knife and stared at her father in disbelief.

"Oh father, you must stop beating a dead horse! You cannot believe that a recently widowed man is someone whom is interested in marrying your spinster daughter." Abel looked up sharply at her.

"Firstly, you are not a spinster. Not for the time being, mind you...and secondly, it is not my intention to push marriage upon a devastated man. I am merely suggesting you provide comfort to a man and a child who desperately require a support system. Everything is not sordid and dark, Emilia. You must learn that every cloud had a silver lining. And when you learn that, perhaps you can pass that information along to the Bawells." Contritely, Emilia looked at her hands and then continued peeling potatoes. Secretly she was pleased that Aaron and Amity were coming. She had been unable to stop thinking about the man, despite his brusque nature. He is a hard man to reach, perhaps due to the circumstances.

"Yes, father," she replied. "What shall I make for supper tomorrow night?"

"Well apparently anything but mutton," Abel jested lightly.

When Aaron and Amity appeared on the veranda of the Troyer home, something seemed different. Amity was no long sulky and angry. She was very quiet and seemed almost out of touch with what was occurring in her presence. Abel introduced her to Evelyn and Collette but she was as disinterested in the girls as Aaron was in Emilia. The entire grouping was a fiasco and Emilia wanted to escape. As the men and children sipped on lemonade on the porch, Emilia put the finishing touches on supper before calling everyone inside. The men seated at both ends of the table, grace was said and Emilia began to serve generous portions of fried beef cutlets, roasted potatoes and corn. Collette passed bread around the table.

"This is excellent, Emilia. You are a wonderful cook," Abel declared, taking a bite of his meal. She smiled at his transparency and he winked subtly in her direction.

"Thank you, father," she replied. She looked expectantly at Aaron but he continued to eat his food, unspeaking. Emilia felt her heart sink. She was expecting too much from this man. She did not know why she felt so drawn to him, why it was so important that he like her but she could not think of anything she wanted more than for him to look at her and say one kind word. Emilia sighed and put her fork onto her plate, her appetite suddenly depleted. She waited for the others to finish their meal before rising to clear away the dishes. Collette and Evelyn rose to help. When the three siblings were in the kitchen, Collette rolled her dark eyes heavenward.

"What a bore!" she exclaimed.

"Shhh!" Emilia hissed at her sister. "Lower your voice immediately!"

"That girl is odd," Evelyn piped up. "She doesn't say anything!"

Emilia turned and glared at her nine-year-old sister.

"Many people would say you are odd because you say too much! Shame on you both! They are guests in our home and we treat them with the respect they deserve. What's more is you do not ever judge a someone for you do not know where they have come from!" Evelyn looked aghast, completely unaccustomed to being reprimanded by Emilia. Her own limpid eyes filled with tears.

"I didn't mean harm" she whispered. "I'm sorry, Emmy. I respect our guests!"

Emilia was filled with remorse as she watched her sister's face but she stood firm.

"When you respect people, you do not speak ill of them behind their backs. I want you to carefully consider your words before you speak from this day forward. You can cause someone a great deal of harm with your language and imagine how ashamed you will feel if that person needed a friend but instead were only met with idle name calling. You two are better than that! You were raised to be charitable and kind. Do not disappoint papa and I." Nodding, both girls shuffled upstairs to avoid any further punishment. As they disappeared, Abel walked into the kitchen.

"You will make a good mother," he told her quietly.

"Did you hear those two?" Emilia asked, placing a dish towel onto the counter, shaking her head in disbelief, purposely ignoring her father's comment. Abel nodded.

"Yes, I heard them. And I heard what you told them."

"Well it's true. They were raised better than that," Emilia said, reaching into the ice box for the cobbler she had made for dessert.

"I heard something else also," Abel said, drawing closer. Emilia glanced up.

"What else did you hear, father?" Abel gently touched her face so she was looking at him. He smiled genuinely, his eyes twinkling with happiness.

"I heard you call me 'papa.'"

Emilia had just finished hanging the wash on the line when she heard a faint knock at the door. Hurriedly, she picked up the basket and rushed inside. Unceremoniously, she threw open the door and her breath caught in her throat.

"Mr. Bawell!" He had been staring blankly into the yard and seemed to snap out of his reverie when Emilia spoke his name.

"Emilia," he nodded. He had a faraway look in his eye and he bit his lip as if in concentration.

"Are you all right?" Emilia questioned, trying to make sense of why he was standing on the doorstep. Unconsciously, her hand swept through her hair, smoothly the flyaway strands.

"No." Emilia stared expectantly at him, waiting for an elaboration which did not materialize. She sighed. He was still determined to be standoffish and she had far too much to do that day than vie for his affection.

"Mr. Bawell, my father is at the shop if you would like to speak with him," Emilia offered. Aaron blinked at her as if he did not comprehend her words.

"No," he said again, in a flat, monotonous way. "I need you."

Emilia's heart fluttered and she shushed it in her head but a smile could not help but find its way to her lips.

"Oh?" she asked with some uncharacteristic coyness. Her smile faded with his very next words.

"My daughter has vanished. I need you to help me find her."

III

Night had fallen and there was still no trace of young Amity. Aaron Bawell sat perfectly still on a straight back chair, as if his soul had floated away from his body. A search party had formed and they had covered all of the hills and valleys in the district but no one had found a sign of the girl.

"She will turn up. She probably just got lost. They will find her," Abel told Aaron soothingly, trying to force his neighbor to eat and drink but Aaron was unhearing, unseeing and seemingly uncaring. The members of the community gathered in the bishop's home, waiting for word and speculating among themselves.

"Who would abduct a small Amish girl?" they wondered. "Our way is peaceful. This is unheard of!"

"She was not abducted," Emilia suddenly said, an epiphany hitting her full force. There was a murmur of skepticism as she began to pace excitedly, her mind racing.

"How can you know that, Emilia? This is commonplace with the English. Kidnapping and such. A stranger must have wandered off with her."

"No one wandered off with her," Emilia told them. "She has not been kidnapped."

"What do you believe happened to her?"

For the first time in hours, Aaron looked up, his once vacant eyes filled with hope.

"Where is my daughter, Emilia?" he begged, his voice hoarse with emotion.

"She went to where her mother is resting."

Amity had been walking for over seven hours, her little legs exhausted as she trekked toward her old district. It was Aaron himself who had found his small daughter, asleep on the side of the dirt road, completely hidden to eyes not searching. Her cheeks were caked in salted tears, her nose completely blocked from the endless crying her journey had seen. Aaron had flown off the carriage before it had come to a complete halt. He scooped up his daughter in strong arms and held her tightly but even that gesture did not wake the child from the depth of her sleep. Swaddling her like an infant, Aaron carefully placed her in the back of the wagon and sat with her as Abel took the reins and began the journey back to Latham District. Emilia sat in the wagon with father and daughter. Assured that Amity was still asleep, Aaron turned to the lovely blonde across from him. She could not make out his face as the wagon was dark and the night, moonless.

"How did you know?" he finally asked her. "How did you know where she had gone?"

Emilia was silent a moment. Ever since she had learned of Beth's death, it was as if a floodgate of memories had taken Emilia over. She began reliving every painful event which occurred from the moment her own mother had passed. When Aaron had arrived on the doorstep that afternoon, Emilia hadn't immediately made the connection but as time went on, it became clearer that Amity had not been taken and instead had run off somewhere. There was only one place the child wanted to be; with her mother. Of course Emilia knew that. That feeling was still very fresh in her own heart.

"I was Amity not too many years ago," Emilia told Aaron. "I understand how she feels."

There was a deep quiet from the other side of the transportation.

"I tried very hard," Aaron finally said.

"It is not easy," Emilia agreed.

"No. It is worse than that. Beth was sick for a great while. I had expected her to pass from when Amity was two years old. But she was a fighter, our Beth. She would get well and then get sick again, well and sick once more, each time getting worse and worse. Her body was failing. Everyone could see it including Beth. Our entire community knew it was only a matter of time. But Amity was just a baby. She only saw her mother. And she had so much hope that her mother would get well." Again, there was silence. Emilia opened her mouth to speak some words of comfort when Aaron took a breath.

"I despised my wife at the end of her life, Emilia. God help me, it's the truth. I loathed the fact that she would not give up and would continue to put our daughter through the trauma of watching her fall ill time and again. I am a despicable person. What kind of man wants his wife to die?" There was a catch in his voice and Emilia swallowed the lump in her own throat.

"The kind of man who cannot bear to watch others suffer," she answered quietly. "A very noble man. A man who loves his daughter so much that it tore him apart to watch her cry day after day for her mama." A man like my father, Emilia thought, her heart swelling with love for the man in the front of the carriage.

"I have been very uncouth to you, Emilia," Aaron suddenly said from the darkness. His voice was gruff.

"You have been grieving," she replied. "I do not consider a grieving man uncouth."

"No. That is not why I have been so uncivilized to you."

Emilia opened her mouth to protest but instead decided to wait for him to continue.

"When Beth found out she was dying, she made me promise to get married immediately so Amity would have a mother. She made numerous suggestions as to who should replace her. I agreed to placate her during her last days but the thought of marrying anyone else, of Amity calling anyone else 'mama' was horrifying and wrong. Some women in my community were overtly suggestive even prior to Beth's passing and when she finally did pass, there were knocks on my door quite literally the next day. That is why I made such a hasty decision to take Amity and leave."

"Ah, you thought I was one of the women vying for position of your wife," Emilia said slowly feeling her face blush crimson. Oh papa! Do you see what your meddling has done now?

"No, that's not what I believed, Emilia. I had seen you at church and you were so lovely, my breath actually halted when I laid eyes upon you. I had never felt that way about anyone. You are so beautiful but in a modest, unassuming form. I saw how well everyone has taken to you, how hard you work and how your sisters adore you. You are everything a man could hope for. I knew I had to stay far away from you. Yet when your father approached me in a neighborly fashion, I could not resist inviting you to supper. I wanted you near but I wanted you far away. Do you understand?"

Emilia almost laughed out loud.

"I understand exactly what you mean," she replied. "And now?"

Out of the dark, a large, calloused hand found hers. An unexpected shiver went up her spine at the touch. She squeezed his palm gently.

"And now the thought of marrying anyone other than you is horrifying and wrong." Aaron squeezed her hand back and for the first time since her mother died, Emilia felt the weight of the world lift off her shoulders.

She was actually happy.

END

AMISH SUNSET

NANCY MANN

116

Chapter I

Rain decorated the grassy fields of Lancaster County. The sky was a cloud grey, the sun remaining absent as the county mourned for the loss of William Bradshire, a carpenter that had been known throughout the county for his kindness and love towards the people around him.

Friends and family had gathered in the county's cemetery for William's funeral, one of the mourners being William's love, Mary Lee Warner. Out of everyone there, Mary was the most damaged from it. William's parents had passed on early in his life due to illnesses and the remaining family he had weren't as close. If anything, Mary was the only one there who truly was family to him.

As Bishop David spoke about his memories with William, Mary thought to herself how God could do such a thing, to take away an innocent being this early in his life. William was only in his mid-twenties, like Mary. He had so much to experience in his life, but it was stripped away from him so early due to the accident.

"If anyone has anything to say, speak now." Bishop David said, stepping back and letting anyone step forward to speak.

There was a long pause, silence being present as Mary thought to herself. Eventually, she took a step forward, standing in front of the casket as she let out a depressed sigh.

"William...had a beautiful soul," Mary said quietly, holding onto a wildflower, "a soul that I have yet to find in any other human being."

Everyone was watching her speak, seeing what Mary had in her hand and what she had to say about William being gone.

"I can't imagine not meeting him in my life...all the memories we've made together...all the laughter, the love...I'm going to miss it." Mary spoke as tears ran down her cheeks. "I don't know if I will find another William in my life."

Some of William's family members began to have tears fall too as they listened to Mary's words about their lost kin. Mary soon stepped back from the casket, having finished speaking on the behalf of William's death. Bishop David soon stepped forward again, wiping some tears from his own eyes.

"Thank you Mary...I will say, before I close in prayer, that it will be difficult to find another William in our lives." Bishop David said to Mary before opening his Bible.

Verses from the Bible were soon spoken out loud, everybody bowing their heads in prayer as Bishop David spoke. While everyone listened, Mary wasn't listening to the verses, in fact, she was in her own mind at this point.

"Why God...why would you take William away from me?" Mary thought to herself. "William didn't even get half way into his life...why would you take him now?"

As she struggled with the idea of William passing on, Bishop David finished reading the verses, quietly speaking the word amen as he closed his Bible, everybody soon leaving the scene of the funeral, letting the casket to be lowered into the grave. While the casket lowered, Mary was the only one present, witnessing her love's final presence on the surface of Earth.

In regards to funeral traditions of the Amish, flowers were not placed on the casket. For Mary though, traditions meant nothing to her in this occasion. She took the wildflower that she was holding in her hand and tossed it down into the undug grave, letting it land on the coffin before the gravediggers began to bury the coffin.

"I love you so much William." Mary said as the coffin soon disappeared from the soil piling on top. Tears continued to fall onto the soil as she left the site of the funeral.

Chapter II

Several years later...the county had returned back to its normal ways, except for Mary. Ever since William passed away, Mary wasn't her old self. Her old cheerful personality had passed on as well, leaving her a closed up, emotionless woman in her mid-twenties.

She tried to return back to a normal life by going to church, seeing if God might be able to help her find peace, but the more she went the church, the more she began to question God. At times, she would find herself being angry at God for taking William away this early in his life. Eventually, Mary stopped going to church, which brought the concern of Bishop David, leading him to go to Mary's home.

Her house was a little way from town, being near one of the farms. She lived in a large house that belonged to William and his parents. Now that William passed on, Mary now owned the house and lived in it by herself.

Bishop David knocked on the front door, waiting for it to be opened. It took a few knocks before the door finally opened, Mary standing there in a stone grey dress.

"Yes?" Mary quietly said, looking at him with her expressionless face.

"May I come in?" Bishop David asked softly, his expression being hopeful that she would accept his request.

Mary let out a quiet sigh before she nodded, stepping out of the way for Bishop David to come in.

"Thank you...Mary." He said, soon walking into her home, looking around.

Mary shut the door behind Bishop David, walking past him and sitting down on a chair in the living room, continuing what she was doing before he knocked. When Bishop David sat down across from her, he noticed that she was knitting a quilt.

"Oh...I see that you've been busy with making a quilt." Bishop David said, giving Mary a gentle smile.

"Quilts. I've been busy making quilts." She said quickly, pointing in the corner to a basket of several quilts.

Bishop David was surprised by the amount of quilts she had made. "That's quite the number of quilts Mary." He said with a small laugh after.

Mary raised her eyebrows as she continued to knit the quilt. "I've found that work is one of the few things that keeps me from thinking about the past." She said softly, not making eye contact with Bishop David.

"Oh...well...if that's what helps you find peace." He said quietly, rubbing the back of his neck before he finally decided to talk about why he wanted to talk to her. "Mary...I'm worried about you."

She heard Bishop David, stopping for a second before she continued knitting the quilt. "Why?" Mary questioned him.

"I'm concerned for you because you haven't been going to church for months." Bishop David finally said, looking at her with a worried expression. "You were always an avid church-goer when William..." He said before realizing what he said, stopping in mid-sentence.

Mary immediately looked up when Bishop David brought up William, her knitting ceasing before she let out a sigh of disbelief escape her lips. She set the quilt and knitting needle down. "Please, do not ever bring up William to me again when comparing me to then and now." Mary said, her voice trembling as she had grown an upset expression.

Bishop David had become silent as he listened to Mary finally speak to him.

"I'm no longer the Mary from then because of the events that happened, and if you want to visit me and tell me how I use to love church and that you're concerned with me not being there on Sundays, then don't even speak, you're wasting your breath." Mary said to him, her eyes staring into his intensely.

Bishop David heard everything she was saying before he let out a sigh of sympathy. "I'm sorry Mary that you're like this...I didn't come here today to chastise you about not attending church. I came here because I'm really concerned for what you've become. I want happiness for you, I want you to have that cheerful personality that everybody knew you for." He said softly, standing up from sitting, looking down at her. "Always remember Mary, we all face events in life that we don't want, but it's all a part of God's plan for something greater."

Mary just glared at him the whole time he spoke, not even acknowledging the things he said. "I would like you to leave."

Bishop David heard her request and nodded softly, walking away from where they were at and leaving the house.

She had watched him leave through the windows before she finally reached for her knitting needles and quilt, continuing to knit as she thought about what he said about God having a plan for everyone. To her, God's plan was killing William and taking away something that she loved most in the world, when she didn't have anyone else.

"Forget God." Mary said to herself quietly, having completely lost faith and love in God.

Chapter III

One stormy night soon had arrived in Lancaster County. Rain had arrived over the town and fields, the sound of sharp pellets hitting the roofs and windows of each building. The window whirled between each building, the sounds of wind wailing could be heard by anyone who was awake.

While the storm stayed present in the county, Mary was asleep in her bed, although she wasn't sleeping soundly. The red-headed woman was having a nightmare, causing her to toss back and forth in her sleep before some sort of sound interrupted her slumber.

KNOCK KNOCK KNOCK

Mary sat right up from her bed like a vampire in a coffin, rubbing her eyes. "What on Earth?" She said to herself, looking around the room as she wondered what caused her to wake up.

KNOCK KNOCK KNOCK

This time, the red-head heard the solution to the noise. "Who could be at my door in the middle of the night?" Mary got out of her bed, wrapping her blanket around herself to cover her nightgown. She made her way down the stairs of her home before seeing the front door. Once she got to the door, she slowly opened it, seeing who it was.

There was a man, about her age, with a young daughter about six-years-old. They were wet from head to toe, shivering as they looked at Mary.

"Please...do you have room in your home for my child and I? We come from far away to Lancaster County...we have no home, no food." The man said, his tone being a desperate one.

Mary had no idea that this was what waited for her on the other side of the door. "I...Well..." She looked at the two before she finally nodded quickly, stepping out of the way.

"Oh thank you...thank you!" The man said happily and emotionally. He quickly moved inside, Mary shutting the door behind the two. Even though they were inside, away from the rain, they still were shivering in the dark home. Mary saw how cold they were and immediately knew what they needed.

She quickly went over to the fireplace in the living room, taking two logs that were on the side of the hearth in a pile and putting them inside the fireplace. After a few attempts of trying to get a fire started, she eventually managed to do so, an orange glow illuminating the living room.

Once the man saw the fire, he moved his daughter close to the fireplace, trying to get her as warm as possible. Mary saw what he was trying to do and quickly went over to the eight-year-old, wrapping her blanket around the child. The man soon began to dry off her daughter while at the same time trying to get her warm.

"There you go...nice and warm now. Away from the cold rain." He said quietly to his daughter, holding her close as he sat in front of the fireplace with her.

The daughter shivered still, but the warmth from the fire and the blanket caused the shivering to decrease as the time went by.

Mary stood behind the two, watching them and making sure that they were okay. "Are you warm enough?" She asked them, having held one of the quilts she had made in her hands to give to the man.

"Yes...thank you kind miss." He said quietly, holding his daughter close before taking the quilt from Mary, wrapping it around himself.

With the two warming themselves up from the fire, Mary decided to grab another quilt for herself before sitting down on her couch. She wrapped the quilt around her body so she could be warm too. Since she now had two "guests" in her home, she didn't want to go upstairs, back to bed, with the knowledge that two strangers were downstairs in her home, two people who she had no idea who they were.

"Maybe they're thieves," Mary thought to herself, studying the two strangers. "Although...she looks pretty young to be a thief." She finally decided to speak up, wanting to figure out who they were. "Where did you two come from?"

The man looked back at her, hearing her question before he began to reply to her. "We came from Somerset County." The man answered, still trying to warm up his daughter.

"Oh...that's far from here." Mary replied, sitting down on her couch, looking at the man.

"It very much is..." The man nodded, looking at her. "Do you know if there's any housing here in Lancaster County?"

Mary heard her question before she shrugged. "I'm not too sure. Are you looking for a place to stay?"

The man nodded, looking down at his daughter. She had fallen into slumber and had a warm expression on her face and had stopped shivering, indicating she was no longer freezing. "Yes."

She heard him and asked some more questions in order to get to know him. "Why Lancaster County? I'm sure there's plenty of other settlements along the way."

"I just," The man began to say, rubbing the back of his neck nervously, "I don't know...I guess I've heard a lot of great things about Lancaster. Figured that it would be a great place for my daughter to grow up in."

Mary nodded when he stated that it'd be a good place for his daughter to grow up in. "Lancaster really is a nice place to grow up in...a good place to start a fam-" she began to say before stopping when she was about to say "family." It reminded her of what she has always wanted to have and that made her think of William and her. "Well, it's a good place to meet nice and caring people."

The man saw her reaction when she was talking about family, but decided not to question it in order to remain polite. "That's good to hear...by the way," the man began to say, looking at her once again, "what is your name?"

She heard him and replied softly. "Mary...my name is Mary Lee Warner."

When the man heard her, he smiled softly. "That's a beautiful name."

Mary smiled softly when he complimented her name. "What about you? What's your name?"

"Robert." He said quietly, before looking down at his daughter, gently stroking her hair. "The little one is Miriam."

Chapter IV

The next morning had arrived, the rain was now gone, the only trace of rain being the puddles in the dirt. Mary decided to help Robert and Miriam out by going down to the church to see Bishop David could help them out.

Entering the church, there were only a few people present in the pews, praying to the Lord about whatever comes to their attention. Bishop David was not preaching, considering it was a Tuesday, so chances were he was at his home.

"Doesn't look like he's here." Mary said, turning around and leading Robert and Miriam out.

"Who are we looking for exactly?" Robert said, holding his daughter's hand as they walked towards Bishop David's house.

"We're looking for David, Lancaster County's bishop. He might be able to help you out with moving here." Mary replied, reaching the bishop's house before knocking on the door. Not too long after the knock, the door opened, Bishop David standing there.

"Mary?" He said, a little surprised. "What brings you here today?"

Mary explained the whole story to him, telling the bishop that Robert and Miriam showed up in the middle of the night, needing a place to stay and that they wanted to move to Lancaster.

"I see..." Bishop David said quietly, scratching his beard as he thought about it. "Unfortunately, there isn't any houses available right now."

Mary heard the news and let out a quiet groan. "So where will they stay if they don't have a home?"

Bishop David heard her before looking at the two, looking at Mary again. "Can I talk to you privately Mary?"

Mary was confused as to why, but nodded as she stepped inside the bishop's house. "What did you want to talk to me about?"

Bishop David looked at her before he let out a quiet sigh. "I wanted to talk to you privately about where they're going to stay. I believe they should continue living at your house until a new house can be built here in the county."

She listened to what he said before hearing his statement about the two staying at her home. "What? No. I can't have people living at my house."

Bishop David gave her a confused look. "Why not? You have one of the biggest houses here in Lancaster County. You're not living with anyone. There's plenty of room in the house for someone."

"Because, I don't have enough food to feed two more people. I don't want to start housing people." Mary was quick to say, folding her arms. "I can't let strangers come into my home and make themselves acquainted to the hou-"

"Mary." Bishop David interrupted, clearly showing he was getting irritated with her. "Enough with the excuses. I'm not going to force you to let them in. I'm only suggesting you give the two of them a home. It's not permanent, but where else are they going to go?" He asked Mary, looking at her with a serious expression. "They can't move into anyone else's home. They all have families, rather large ones too."

She listened to him, looking into his eyes as she thought about everything he was saying. Bishop David was right in many ways. Most families in the county had large families, homes that were already crowded. With Mary's house, it was just her. He even said that it wasn't permanent, so it'd be something that Mary didn't have to deal with for too long.

"I guess...I could have them stay for a little while." Mary finally admitted, realizing that she could be a little generous.

"Thank you Mary." Bishop David said before leading her back outside, now facing Robert. "We will discuss adding a house whenever I meet my colleagues. Until we can get a house added to the county, you'll have to stay with Mary for the time being."

Robert listened to what Bishop David said, nodding softly. "Okay, thank you."

Bishop David smiled softly, heading back into the house before closing the door.

Robert and Miriam turned toward Mary, looking at her. "So...are we going to back to the nice lady's house?" Miriam asked her father.

Mary heard her and couldn't help but smile. "Yes...yes you are."

Robert watched the two interact before he couldn't help but smile, seeing this stranger being so nice to his daughter.

"Alright. Let's head back to the house so I can get a room prepped up for you two." Mary said, clapping her hands together when she knew what she needed to do.

Chapter V

A couple of months passed by in Mary's household. The two strangers that had showed up on her doorstep were now friends of hers, having brightened up the household little by little. As Mary got to know Robert, he started feeling more and more comfortable around him, the two even joking around with each other.

With Miriam, she started to look up towards Mary as a mother figure, every now and then the little girl called Mary mom. Mary would hear this and laugh, finding it humorous that Robert's daughter called her mom.

While everyone was getting along just fine, Mary started to remember William again, every time she looked at Robert. There was something about Robert that reminded her of William. It might've been the way he made her laugh or the way he showed kindness to people. Whatever it was, Mary could see William through Robert, which made her think about if she found another William in her life.

It was now 6 PM and Robert and Miriam had finished eating dinner with Mary. When they finished, Robert decided to take Miriam to bed, since she started dozing off during dinner. Once she was in bed, she was out cold.

"She must've been really tired today. Miriam never goes to bed this early." Robert said, walking back into the kitchen. "I don't blame her...she didn't sleep that well last night."

"Oh poor thing." Mary said, cleaning the dishes in the sink. "I hope she rests well tonight."

"She probably will." Robert said, walking over before leaning against the counter. "So...what do you want to do?"

Mary continued to wash the dishes before she stopped, soon looking at him. "What do you mean?"

"Well I mean...Miriam is in bed early. Do you want to go out for a walk?" Robert replied, looking at her and waiting to hear an answer.

She looked at him before looking down at the dishes, thinking about his offer before setting the plates down. "I would enjoy that."

He smiled brightly before he walked out of the kitchen, planning on getting his jacket.

It didn't take long before the two were on an adventure, walking around the county in the early evening. The sky was an vibrant orange, the sun easing itself behind the hills.

"Wow...that's a beautiful sunset." Robert said softly, looking at it.

"It sure is." Mary said quietly, looking at it before she looked at Robert. With the two of them having grown closer, she soon started to think more in regards of making their relationship a bit more than friends. "Can I show you something?"

Robert heard her, turning his head and looking at her before he smiled softly. "Yeah of course."

Mary smiled brightly before leading him into the woods, walking in a certain direction. As for Robert, he wasn't sure where she was taking him, which made him a little nervous. Eventually, the two arrived in a rather large open area in the woods, a grass area that was decorated with wildflowers.

"Wow..." Robert quietly said to himself, stepping forward and starting to walk towards the flowers. "They're beautiful."

Mary stood behind Robert, watching his response before walking with him again. "I know. I love coming to this place. It reminds me of so many happy memories." She said before she began to lay down in the grass, looking at the sky that had become as orange as a Doris Longwing Butterfly's wing.

Robert watched what she did before he followed her actions, lying next to her as the two watched the sky. "You have quite the spot...especially one that you value." He smiled softly, relaxing on the grass.

The two watched the sky for a few, enjoying the time to relax with each other. Eventually, Robert spoke up, a question that had been resonating within him.

"How come you didn't want to let us live with you a few months ago?" He quietly said, still looking at the sky, some clouds gently moving along in the sky.

Mary heard him and gave him a confused look. "What do you mean?"

"You were talking to Bishop David the morning after the rainstorm. You told him that you didn't want anyone staying at the house because you didn't have enough food and didn't want housing people. Part of me though doesn't believe that."

Mary listened to what Robert was saying, her expression staying confused before her expression became more of a look of hesitant.

"There's something more than not enough food and not wanting to house people huh? You don't have to tell me, but just know I'm here if you want to talk." Robert said quietly, wanting to assure that she could trust him.

She listened to what he said before she began biting her own lip, thinking to herself before she let out a quiet sigh. "There is...there's a lot more to it. I think it's fair that you should know."

He heard her response to his question and turned onto his side, looking at her now as she began to speak about what the reason for not wanting anyone to live with her.

"It all has to do with a man I loved...a man named William." Mary said quietly.

Chapter VI

William Bradshire...a carpenter of Lancaster County. Most of the county knew him as the kind man who cared about everyone around him, even the ones who didn't care for him. William was the prime example of what it means to follow Christ's footsteps. He showed a strong love towards God, helped out around his community, showed love towards everyone, taught the youth about the Bible, and that's just the peak of the iceberg.

Sometimes in life though, bad things can occur that change one's life. For William, it was losing his parents at the age of eighteen. With his parents gone, he now owned the house, but that meant nothing to William. For a long time, he had struggled with the fact that his parents were gone, but during this time, he still continued to help people, having put them first before himself.

A great example of William putting others first was one cold, dark night. There was a knock on his door, the knock having echoed the entire silent household. When William opened his front door, he found a shivering girl his age, looking up at him. This girl was Mary.

The young girl had ran away from home, angry at her parents and her peers around her community. She was looking for a place to stay, which was she ended up on William's doorstep, a stranger to him. William was caring enough to immediately let her in; he even allowed her to stay as long as she needed. Even though she could've left any time, she found herself a priceless friendship.

Eventually, as time progressed, the redhead soon fell in love with William, the same happening with the boy. The two ended up revealing their love for each other when they discovered and rested in the grass area in the woods with the wildflowers. Ever since then, they were two peas in a pod.

As time progressed, they became closer and closer, almost being one soul. Mary began helping out in the community with him while developing a strong love of God since William introduced her to Him. Eventually, William decided that he was going to ask Mary for her hand in marriage, but his colleagues asked for his help in finishing the construction of a barn.

Unfortunately, William never had the chance to pop the question due to the accident. While he was watching his colleagues raise one of the barn walls up by pulling it up with ropes, the ropes snapped and the wall soon fell on William, his chances of escaping the wall very low with how fast the whole situation took. Sadly, William didn't survive the heavy barn wall crushing him.

Word soon got out around the county about William dying from the accident, which Mary soon heard about. She was devastated, crushed, her heart torn into pieces for the loss of her one true love.

After William had passed, Mary was given the house, considering she basically lived there and was a member of the community. During this time, Mary closed herself off from the rest of the world, locking herself away in her home, mourning the loss of William. She even decided to not let anyone into the house after the loss in order to keep the house peaceful, like it was when William and her were in it.

Even in the present, Mary still has nightmares about the whole incident, nightmares that remind her of the loss of William.

"If only I were there to stop him...to get him out of the way...If only I were there...he'd still be alive."

Chapter VII

Once Mary finished telling Robert the story, she had developed some tears from the memory of William's death.

"Now you know why I don't let anyone into the house...I know...it sounds insane, for the girlfriend of someone who has departed to keep the house like a temple. You must think I'm crazy..." Mary said quietly, wiping her tears.

"Oh no..." Robert said, looking at her. "I don't think you're insane at all...I can see why you value the house so much. All the memories with William...the laughter...the peace...everything about it...you don't want anyone to ruin this place for you." He said softly, gently resting his hand on hers. "I'm sorry...I didn't know this was the reason why you didn't want us here."

Mary heard him and finally broke down, tears rolling down her cheeks as she covered her face with her hands, muffled crying heard behind it. Robert reached for her and wrapped his arms around her, holding her close as he embraced her.

"Shhh...it's okay...Mary." Robert quietly said, stroking her hair gently to calm her down. "It's okay..."

After years of suppressing the memories of William and her, the pain she has endured from remembering his death, the many tears she had held back, she finally broke down and let her tears flow.

"I miss him so much...every day I wish I could see him again...tell him that I wish I could've saved him from the wall...I wish I could've done something." She said, pressing her face against Robert's shoulder as she shook from her crying.

"You couldn't do anything Mary...you had no idea that would happen..." Robert said softly, continuing to hold her close as she cried against him. "Look on the bright side...with William having a strong love for God, he's finally in Heaven where he can be with God...walk along with him...talk to him...laugh with him."

With Robert's words entering Mary's ears, it made her cry more. He was right in the sense that she wouldn't have known and that he's in a better place now. Her heart ached as she recalled all the memories of William from when they met to his death. All the memories were mainly happy and ones that would make her laugh whenever she looked back to them. Even though William was gone, she remembered one thing...William lives on through her. The memories, the house, the ideology, everything that William was made up of lives on through Mary. With this thought, she felt like she could finally get over the tragedy of losing William and achieve peace.

"Thank you...Robert...Thank you." Mary said quietly, looking up at him with tears in her eyes.

Robert looked down at her, confused as to why she was telling him thank you. "For what?" He laughed gently, wiping the tears away from her eyes.

"For saying all of those things about William and I...I've spent all these years holding onto William's tragedy and blaming myself for not being able to help him, but now I can finally find peace and let go of the tragedy...thank you...Robert." She finally said, looking at him as she gently reached up, stroking his cheek before she finally decided to lean in, kissing him gently.

Robert was caught off guard with the kiss, his eyebrows raising as she held her in his arms. Eventually, she broke the kiss, resting her head on his should. "Let's go back home...it's getting late." Mary said quietly, her eyes now closed.

Even though Robert had thought about pushing their relationship to another level, there was something that was holding him from reaching that level, something that had followed him from his previous home.

Chapter VIII

———————

Many weeks had passed by since Mary told Robert about her past. Mary was in a much brighter mood, slowly building herself up again by socializing with people, going to church again, which made Bishop David happy, and she started wearing colorful clothes again.

Robert was thinking about what Mary had done in the wildflower area in the woods on the porch. He wanted to moved towards the next step, but the past was catching up with him.

"Hey!" Mary called out, coming up to the house with Miriam. "We've got dinner!"

He snapped back into reality, smiling gently when he saw the two. "Oh...that's wonderful. Looks delicious." Robert said, standing up and helping them take the food inside the house.

"I decided to cook something special for you...to thank you for helping me return back to my old self again."

Robert smiled and chuckled nervously, rubbing the back of his neck. "Oh...you don't have to do that."

"But papa," Miriam spoke out, looking at him, "look at the food! It looks delicious! At least let mom...Mary cook it for me."

Both Robert and Mary laughed at Miriam's comment, Mary picking her up and holding her.

"Okay, well if Robert doesn't want his special dinner, then I'll cook it for you." She said, walking in with the child.

"That'd be fantastic!" Miriam exclaimed happily.

Robert followed behind the two with the groceries, his expression being lost in thought as he thought about the past.

———————

Dinner time soon arrived, everyone now seated at the table as they waited for Mary to come in with the special dinner.

"Whatever she's cooking, it smells delicious." Miriam said, excited to eat.

In a matter of minutes, Mary came out with a cooked turkey, the skin being a golden crisp.

Even though Robert wasn't asking for a special dinner, he was impressed with how the turkey came out. "Wow, looks really good Mary."

She smiled brightly, setting the plate down. "Well I'm glad you like it so much. I've got more coming out. I cooked some corn, made so mashed potatoes, have some greens." Mary explained to them as she walked back into the kitchen.

It took a few trips for her before she finally could sit down at the table with the two. "Alright, dig in." Mary said, taking her knife and fork, cutting into the turkey and scooping up a little bit of everything.

The dinner that they had all together was nice. Lots of laughter, lots of compliments, complete joy filled the room between Miriam and Mary, although Robert was most of the time quiet. After dinner, Miriam decided to go play with her doll in the living room while Mary and Robert were in the kitchen, cleaning the dishes.

While they were in there, Robert remained quiet, lost in his thoughts as he kept trying to shake it off. It didn't take too long though for Mary to see something was bothering him.

"You've been awfully quiet this evening...is there something wrong?" Mary asked him, continuing to wash the dishes.

"No." Robert said vaguely, not wanting to get into what was bothering him.

"You sure?" She said softly, looking at him. "You seem like you're thinking really hard about something."

"Don't worry about it." Robert said to her, trying to avoid explaining his thoughts.

Eventually, Mary let out a quiet sigh before setting her dish down, turning toward Robert.

"You know if something is troubling you, you can te-" Mary began to say to him.

"Drop it." Robert said harshly, looking at her for a few quick seconds before he finally set his plate down, shaking his head. "Just forget it...I'm going to bed." He said, leaving the kitchen and walking upstairs.

Mary was shocked by the way Robert reacted, considering it wasn't normal for Robert to be this way.

Miriam heard the commotion from the living room, looking at Mary. "Is papa upset about something?" She said with a concerned voice.

Mary heard Miriam and shook her head. "Don't worry about it dear. He just needs some time to himself."

Chapter IX

Robert currently laid in Mary's bed upstairs, his eyes closed as he tried sleeping. He didn't mean to snap at Mary, but considering his thoughts were getting to him, it was bound to happen. As he attempted to sleep, he soon felt something lay next to him, which interrupted his slumber. He opened his eyes and turned to look and see if it was Mary.

Of course, he was right in this situation. Mary was in her nightgown, having crawled in bed with Robert, getting cozy. Once he saw it was Mary, he returned back to his previous position, his back facing her. Still trying to avoid breaking the news to Mary, he soon felt her arms around his stomach, her body soon pressing against his back.

"What's going on with you? You're usually not like this." She said softly, resting her head against his back.

"I don't know Mary...I don't know." Robert said quietly, his eyes still closed.

"I feel like you do know Robert." Mary finally said. "I just feel like you don't want to tell me what you're thinking of."

He heard what she said, but didn't reply to it. The only thing he did was sit in silence with his eyes closed, trying to fall into slumber.

"You know I'm here if you want to tell me what's bothering you. I think it'd be healthy if you did though because you won't get any sleep with you thinking about whatever you're thinking. I know from experience." Mary quietly said, now closing her eyes as she rested her head against his back.

Robert listened to what she was saying before he let out a quiet sigh, trying to think about how he would explain his thoughts to her. Eventually, he decided to be straightforward with her.

"You know why I decided to move to Lancaster County?" He asked Mary quietly.

She merely shook her head against his back, indicating that she didn't know why he moved here. "Aside from finding a new home, no I don't."

Robert listened to what she had to say before he continued. "I left my previous home because my wife walked out on Miriam and I."

When Mary heard this, her eyes opened up and she sat up, looking down at him. "What? That's horrible! Why would she do that?"

Once Mary sat up, Robert turned so that he was laying on his back, now looking up at her. "To be honest...maybe I married the wrong person. She just...everything seemed fine to me. She was a good mother, I was a good father, we lived a happy life, but then one day..." He said before stopping, thinking back to that day before telling Mary what happened.

"Sara?" He called out, looking around his home. "Where are you?

While he walked around the house, Miriam watched him, not understanding what was going on. "Papa? What's going on?"

"I can't find mom. She's gone." Robert said, his tone being a little more scared. "Maybe she left something saying where she went. Yeah...she leaves notes."

"Maybe...I'll help you try and find something" Miriam said, getting off of the couch before walking around their home, trying find anything that could lead to the mystery of where Robert's wife went.

Eventually, Miriam found a note that had fallen on the side of the bed. "Papa!" She called out. "I found a note!"

Robert immediately ran into the room, seeing the note in Miriam's hand. He took the note from her and began reading it. Although the hope he had on his expression when he found the note soon faded the more he continued to read it. In fact, he soon had become emotionless from what was written on the note.

"What does it say papa?" Miriam asked, looking up at him.

Robert finished reading the note, looking down at Miriam before folding the note in half, tucking it into his pocket. "Don't worry about it sweetheart. I think though...we need to move away from this county."

When Miriam heard this, she was completely confused. "Why? Why do we need to move?"

He heard her before he picked her up, looking around the house one last time. "Because I think we will find somewhere else that'll be better for the both of us."

"We basically left the county with nothing but the clothes on our back. I couldn't stand living in the same county as her and live in a house that we lived in together." Robert said quietly, looking at Mary as he finished explaining his story. "Would you stay in the same place if you found out your love left you and your child for someone else?"

When Mary heard this, she let out a depressed sigh. "No...I don't think I would." She said quietly. "Is that what's been on your mind today?"

Robert heard her before nodding softly. "I've been thinking about it for a long time now...I've wanted to move onto the next step in our relationship, but...I fear that something would happen again...I fear the odds of you walking out on us."

Once Robert said that, Mary spoke up in a more serious tone. "Robert...look at me."

Robert did as told and look into her eyes, seeing what she would say.

"I would never do that...ever in my life." Mary said, looking at him as she gently rested her hand on his cheek. "I wouldn't do something to hurt you and Miriam...I love you both, with all my heart." She said to him before she gently kissed him, breaking it soon after before resting her head on his chest. "You don't need to worry about me every walking out on you two...I care about you two so much that my heart aches. I wouldn't even think about walking out on you two."

When Robert heard this, he let out a relieved sigh, his arms wrapping around her and hugging her against him. "I love you so much Mary..."

"I love you too Robert..."

THE END

The Painted Lake

ABBY BARKER

Emma hadn't missed a sunrise since she was old enough to help Mama with the laundry, with the exception of that day last winter when she woke up with a cold that kept her bedridden. To Emma, the sun peeking over grassy horizon signified the beginning of all things: life, journeys, and the potential that comes with each new day. Waking up after sunrise would be like turning down a message of encouragement from God, which Emma couldn't bear to waste, so she woke every day at the crack of dawn ready to face whatever challenges arose and accept all graces given to her. This was a schedule that she intended to keep for all time.

This morning, though, she almost missed it. The night before she spent tossing around in her bed, sometimes staring at the ceiling, sometimes the wall, but almost never the backs of her own eyelids. She was restless, but careful to move softly as not to wake up her pig-tailed younger sister, Abigail, who would not have to feel this nervousness for another handful of years, if she would even feel it then. If it was up to Emma, she would have been baptized years ago, but Mama insisted that she take some time to "test her faith." But she already knew her faith to be true; in her heart she knew it. That was enough for her, why wasn't it enough for Mama? This was the last thought she had before finally drifting off to sleep just before dawn.

It seemed as if no time had passed when Abigail gently nudged her sister awake just as the sun began its morning assent.

"Emma! Em!" she half-whispered, "It's today. You've got to get ready. You've got to go so you can hurry up and get back to tell me everything! What do you think Auntie Willa is like? You have to drive a car!"

Emma couldn't match her sister's excitement, but Abigail was right about one thing: The sooner she left, the sooner the month in the city she and Mama had agreed on would be over and she could come home.

"Abigail, please!" she snapped, "I hardly got any sleep and I have plenty of time to pack my bag." She wouldn't have to pack much. In her letters, Auntie Willa insisted they would go shopping the moment she got settled in.

"The clothing is part of the experience," wrote Auntie Willa, "you won't need your bonnet in the city!"

Emma frowned as she rolled away from her sister and turned her back on the dawn. She wanted to stay in bed forever, but she'd settle for five more minutes.

***

After completing her morning chores, Emma changed into a simple, but flattering white linen dress she thought was suitable for traveling. She looked at herself in the mirror as she brushed her long, sun-streaked hair, trying to untangle the knots on her head and in her stomach. A furrowed brow shaded her wide, hazel eyes and her dusty pink lips were downturned in a nervous frown. Each stroke of the brush brought her a little comfort, but not much. There was a lot to be nervous about. She had never met Auntie Willa and they had only spoken through letters. Mama, while she couldn't contact Auntie Willa herself, suggested that Emma reach out before she left on rumspringa. If she had to leave her home, Emma thought, she might as well try to stay with a family member while she's away. Even if that family member left on rumspringa herself 19 years ago and was the only one of her friends not to return home.

Since Emma wasn't yet an official member of the church, she was allowed to write to her excommunicated aunt, but she did so begrudgingly and only at her mother's expressed wishes. Emma could tell that Mama missed her sister, which helped assuage her reluctance to reach out. If Mama still cared for her, she couldn't be all bad. Even so, that first letter was tough for Emma to write. It read:

Dear Auntie Willa,

We've never met before but Mama says you're her sister, which makes you my aunt. She says you used to look just like her, but your hair was always wilder. I have many aunts and uncles here at home, but you're the only one who lives in the city. Mama said it would be a good idea to write you even though you're not with the church anymore because I'm eighteen and she wants me to see the English world before I'm baptized. If I had it my way, I'd already be baptized by now but Mama thinks it's important to face temptation, and deny it, before I make my decision. If I already know there's nothing that could tempt me more than the Will of God, why should I bother with rumspringa? You're probably not the right person to ask.

Your niece,

Emma Byler

Emma was surprised by how kind Auntie Willa seemed in her reply. She told Emma how excited she was to hear from her oldest niece and that she missed the family "something fierce." She also said that she agreed with Mama that seeing how the other half lives, especially if Emma was going to choose to stay with the church, was incredibly important. The way she said "if" put Emma on edge, but she couldn't help but like her aunt after reading the rest of the letter. Auntie Willa wrote enthusiastically and earnestly, offering up personal details about herself (she had an apartment in Chicago with a collie-mix named Charlie), and ended almost every other sentence with an exclamation point. Eventually, Auntie Willa asked Emma to come stay with her for a while.

Emma instinctively put the brush back on the vanity in front of her before remembering the open suitcase next to her. She picked the brush back up and packed it away. Auntie Willa was already on her way. She offered to drive down from Chicago to pick Emma up since no one in her family owned a car, and their horse and buggy wouldn't be able to make the journey to the city. In her letters, Auntie Willa kept referring to it as a "road trip" in an attempt to make the long ride sound more fun, but Emma had never been farther from home than the next town over and the idea of sitting in a car, another thing she had never done, for hours on end was daunting. Just as she zipped up her bag she heard the sound of Auntie Willa's car pulling up to the house. She sat on her bed with the bag in her lap for a few minutes before meeting her aunt in person for the first time.

When Emma finally walked into her family's kitchen, Auntie Willa was sitting at the table with a cup of water that Abigail brought her. She was wearing a bright red t-shirt tucked into a bright, floral-print skirt that brushed her ankles. Her curly, chestnut hair had apparently never lost it's wildness, but was clipped back in a twist that made it look like the strands were trying to escape. She and Emma had the same eyes, which were staring happily at her from across the room. Mama couldn't see any of this while she stood at the sink washing dishes and her back turned to Auntie Willa.

"Emma!" she yelled, jumping out of her chair and almost knocking over the water, "Emma, I'm so frickin' excited to finally see your pretty face!"

Mama bristled and Abigail stifled a laugh at Auntie Willa's objectionable language. Emma just stood stock-still as Auntie Willa rounded the kitchen table, arms outstretched like a bird taking flight, and encircled her in an enthusiastic hug.

"Emma, we're going to have so much fun. I mean, of course you're going to be doing some very valuable thinking and learning, too," she shot a careful glance at her sister, "but that doesn't mean it won't also be tons of fun!"

This made Mama briskly dry her hands on her apron, step away from the sink and pivot towards the hugging pair.

"Now you listen, Willa. Emma is staying with you because I think it's a necessary part of a young person's life to look the world straight in the eyes, knowing everything they need to know about their choice, and say 'My priorities lie with God.' It's not about fun. It's about free choice and true faithfulness. I know you clearly don't see it that way considering the path you've chosen, but Emma isn't like you, Willa. She's steadfast and faithful and knows exactly what she's doing."

Auntie Willa was taken aback, but her arm never left Emma's shoulders.

"Jodie, please. I took this decision just as seriously as you did. I just used me 'free choice' a different way is all. I'm sorry that meant things had to turn out the way they did, but it was my choice. Just like this will be Emma's. So if Emma wants to have fun, we're gonna have fun! And if she doesn't, well, what are the odds of that?"

She gave Emma a subtle wink and playful jab at her side, knocking her a little off balance. She regained her footing and spoke up the newly found courage that having her aunt's support provided.

"If it were up to me I wouldn't even be going. Mama, you asked me to do this, so I'm going to do it, but you can't ask me not to have fun. You have to trust me to do the right thing. I don't plan on doing anything in Chicago that I wouldn't do here."

Auntie Willa scoffed gently at this.

"Sweetie, I wouldn't say that. Even riding the elevator up to my apartment is going to be something you wouldn't do here, but I get what you're saying. You and your mother both can rest assured knowing that I would never make you do something you weren't up for. Cross my heart."

She made an "X" in the air over her chest with her right index finger, but Mama didn't look convinced with her arms crossed over her own chest.

"You have to trust me to do the right thing," Emma interjected through the tension.

"Sweetheart, of course I trust you." Mama walked over to her daughter and embraced her. "I know it doesn't seem like it at the moment, but I'm proud of you and grateful that you're doing this. God will guide you. As long as you follow your heart and His word you'll make it through."

She kissed Emma on the top of her head and reluctantly let her go.

"I love you Emma."

"I love you too, Mama. Don't worry about me. I'll make the most of it."

Emma then walked over to her sister and gave her a hug goodbye while she chattered away about clothes, boys, and Navy Pier. She tried to soak up as much of Abigail's excitement as she could before picking up her bag and walking out the door. Mama and Abigail followed them out to the car. When she saw the vehicle, Abigail let out an excited scream and ran over to it.

"It's red!" she yelled back at Mama and Emma, as if she thought they couldn't see it yet. Emma approached more cautiously. It seemed safe enough, by the looks of it, but she knew it could move ten times as fast as any buggy. She imagined the car being pulled along by two of her family's horses and allowed herself a small smile. Auntie Willa offered to help Emma with her bag just as she got close enough to run her fingers along the cool, smooth surface of the car. The trunk popped open on it's own and made Emma jump. Auntie Willa dangled the keys in front of Emma's surprised face.

"Cool, huh?" she said with a grin. Emma only smiled back and nodded. "Well, it's time to hit the road. If you forgot anything we can just pick it up when we get into the city. Bye, Abigail! Bye, Jodie! I'll try to get her back here in one piece!"

Auntie Willa opened the passenger side door for Emma and she slipped inside. She watched her aunt walk around the car to her own side and hop in, flashing Emma a faux-nervous smile. Emma watched her aunt pull the seatbelt around her body and clip it into the buckle.

She took the cue and, after a little bit of fumbling, was safely buckled in. Auntie Willa put the key in the ignition and the car started with a low roar.

"You ready, Em? No turning back now!"

Emma didn't know if she was ready, but she knew she had to be.

"Yes, Auntie Willa. Let's go."

"That's the spirit!" Auntie Willa replied joyously as she pressed a button next to her to open the front two windows. "Wave to your mom and sister. They're gonna miss you!"

Emma stuck her hand out the open window and looked back at her family standing outside. Abigail could barely contain herself as she fidgeted from foot to foot waving frantically. Mama was her opposite, standing tall and still, neither happy nor unhappy about seeing her oldest daughter drive away to Chicago. Emma pulled her hand back inside just as the car began to move. Her stomach lurched, but the feeling receded the farther they drove from home. Auntie Willa turned on the radio and started humming along. Emma kept her eyes locked on the road in front of them, watching her neighbor's homes fly by out of the corner of her eye. Auntie Willa's words echoed in her mind. No turning back now! She was tempted to turn around to see what her house looked like from this far away, but she took those words literally. There will be time to turn around later, she reminded herself, but this was the beginning of a new journey and she was determined to face it head on.

***

The view outside Emma's window slowly morphed from just ripened soy and cornfields to suburban neighborhoods filled with cookie cutter homes and chain grocery stores. She spent the first hour or so of the drive silently watching the world around her change and she felt herself changing, just a little bit, with it. From the safety of the car she was slowly immersed in this new world and allowed herself to become accustomed to it, but she didn't know what to expect when she stepped out.

Auntie Willa had been mostly silent up until now. She happily sang to herself and understood that Emma was the type to quietly take things in before wanting to talk about them, but Auntie Willa was not that type and after an hour of quiet she had about reached her breaking point.

"Are you getting excited? I remember sitting on the edge of my seat about to burst when I left home for the first time."

"I guess I'm...surprised? I thought it would be harder to leave than it was. I thought things would feel more alien, but after passing through all of these towns that look the same it's starting to feel familiar. Does that make sense?"

'Totally! I was blown away by the first Target I saw, but by the ninth or tenth it definitely lost its mystery. Don't you worry, though, Chicago is gonna knock your socks off. I've lived there for almost two decades now and it still takes my breath away when I'm driving toward that skyline. I'm definitely gonna take you to the planetarium. You won't get a better view of the city, or the universe, from anywhere else. I swear, it'll change your life."

She agreed to go on this trip to reassure herself and her family that she wanted her life to stay the same. She hadn't given any thought to how she might come home changed. This thought both scared and excited Emma. For the first time, she allowed herself to think of the experience not just as a trial, but also as an adventure.

"I think I'd like that. Back at home the sky is filled with millions of stars at night. After dinner Abigail and I sometimes go out into the yard and lie down to look up at them. I know that most of them already have names, but we'd lie there and come up with names of our own. I usually picked names of people from the Bible. It's comforting to think God's people are looking down on us, but Abigail always named the stars after boys she likes," Emma giggled at the memory and Auntie Willa followed suit.

"You won't see many stars in Chicago. The sky's mostly filled with planes and helicopters, but you'll be able to see all sorts of things at the planetarium. All the stars named after your sister's crushes and then some!"

Emma tried to imagine how they got all the stars to fit inside one building when the entire skyline of Chicago rose up out of the rode in front of her. She'd never seen it before but she knew it couldn't be anything else. Auntie Willa glanced over at Emma and saw her eyes grow wide.

"Awesome, isn't it? Just you wait."

This feeling was not what Emma expected. She wanted to know what it felt like to be amongst those buildings, and all the people who live in them. She wanted to know how it felt to be a part of something so massive and seemingly intangible. The buildings look small on the horizon, but Emma was still struck by their size. She was so caught up imagining how it would feel to sit on top of the tallest building in Chicago and see the landscape change backward from city, to suburb, to home that she almost forgot she'd planned to go back.

***

Auntie Willa had prepped her for the elevator, but she still gripped the railing with white knuckles when it began its assent. Auntie Willa lived on the nineteenth floor of a high-rise with two bedrooms and a sweeping view of Lake Michigan. One bedroom was Auntie Willa's and Charlie had unofficially occupied the other until the day before. He was a little put out when Auntie Willa dragged his bed and toys out into the living room, but immediately changed his tune when he met Emma. She didn't even have a chance to realize that she'd never been this high up before Charlie bombarded her with doggy kisses. Emma's family didn't own any official pets, just their horses and some chickens, but she immediately warmed up to him.

"Charlie likes you! I knew he would," cooed Auntie Willa.

"I like him, too! We've never had a dog," Emma replied, scratching Charlie behind the ears.

"Well you do now. Mi perro es tu perro!"

"What?"

"Oh that's just a little Spanish for you. It means 'my dog is your dog.' I can teach you a little while you're here if you'd like."

Emma didn't know that Auntie Willa could speak another language. She was impressed by how worldly her aunt was, but then remembered that focusing her attention on things like that is what drew Auntie Willa away from the church in the first place.

"Maybe, but I don't know what good Spanish would do me back home."

It was clear Auntie Willa didn't agree, but she refrained from pushing the matter.

"Why don't you get settled in your room? Maybe hang up some of the clothes you brought, take a shower, and I'll order up some Chinese food. You ever have Chinese food? Probably not, but you'll love it. I swear!"

"Okay," was all Emma could muster. She had only ever eaten what Mama or their neighbors had cooked for her. The idea of "ordering" food was as unfamiliar as "Chinese," but she was uncomfortable denying Auntie Willa's hospitality. She took her bag into the spare room and began to unpack before cautiously figuring out how to work the shower.

When she got out of the bathroom she found a warm looking pair of sweatpants and a baggy t-shirt waiting for her on her bed.

"I know you probably brought a nightgown with you," Auntie Willa yelled from the living room, "but trust me, there's nothing cozier than a hand-me-down pair of sweatpants that are too big for you."

Not one to protest, she pulled on the black pair of pants and the shirt that said "Chicago Marathon 2013" on the front and met Auntie Willa in the living room where a feast of little white boxes, black plastic containers, and a mountain of fortune cookies was waiting for her.

"I didn't know what you liked so I got a little bit of everything. Plus, I told them we were having a party so they'd give me extra fortune cookies. Dig in!" She handed Emma a plate, a pair of chopsticks, and a fork just in case.

Between surprisingly delicious bites of fried rice and sesame chicken, Emma asked her aunt about the t-shirt.

"Did you run a marathon, Auntie Willa?"

"Ha! I just bought ten pounds of Chinese food. What do you think? No, my ex-boyfriend gave me that shirt while we were dating."

Emma was suddenly uncomfortable about the idea of wearing a man's shirt, and Auntie Willa could see that.

"Don't worry, girly, he hasn't warn that shirt in years so it practically never belonged to him in the first place."

This reassured Emma enough that she continued to wear the shirt but now she had more questions.

"Auntie Willa, how many boyfriends have you had?"

"Well that depends. I've officially had three serious boyfriends, but I've casually dated quite a few more."

This took Emma aback. Mama met Papa at a Sunday evening sing and that was that. The girls at home almost always end up marrying the first boy who takes them home in his buggy. The idea that Auntie Willa had dated more than one man, had even worn their clothes, shocked her. She wondered how many other men's t-shirts she had in her closet, but she didn't dare ask.

"Wow," she replied, "I've never even held hands with a boy."

Auntie Willa chuckled kindly, "Well let's see what we can do about that, huh?"

This made Emma blush wildly and spoon too much rice into her mouth to keep from having to respond.

***

Auntie Willa wasted no time fulfilling her promise to take Emma to the planetarium. The very next day, after gently insisting that Emma borrow some more of her clothes and that she "leave the bonnet at home, girly!" they hopped in a cab and made their way to the museum.

The Adler Planetarium sat out on its own at the tip of a peninsula that jutted way out into Lake Michigan. Driving towards the impressive domed building gave Emma the same sensation as when she first saw the Chicago skyline. She couldn't wait to get inside to see where they kept all the stars, but after the cab dropped them off at the entrance Auntie Willa put her hand on Emma's shoulder to stop her from immediately sprinting up the stairs to the front doors.

"Hold up! Turn around first. Don't you want to see what I was talking about?"

Emma turned and saw the same skyline that awed her from a distance magnified and close enough to touch. That impressive massiveness that she felt fifty miles away was now right on top of her. The beautiful weight of the city was balanced on her small shoulders and she loved it. This feeling was enough to cause a small chip in Emma's resolve to return home, and this frightened her. She spun around on her heal, as if not being able to see the skyline made it not exist. She wasted no time climbing the stairs to the planetarium now. She relied on the familiarity of the stars to remind her of why she wanted to go home, but she didn't count on what else she would find inside.

***

After wandering around the exhibits for a while, taking in every fact about space, the stars, and especially the Sun that she could find, Auntie Willa suggested that they sit for a while and see a show. They decided on one called Skywatch Live! which showed how the night sky above Chicago would look if the city turned off all of its lights. This one interested Emma the most. She wanted to see how different the sky is here as opposed to at home.

Soon after they took their seats in the huge, domed theater the lights dimmed and the starry Chicago sky was projected above them. Emma had to stifle a gasp as every star she'd ever seen and more swirled above them. She was loath to admit it to herself, but it was almost more magical than the real night sky at home. Wrapped up in the tableau unfurling in front of her, she was caught off guard when a voice projected across the audience.

"Welcome, everybody! Thanks for coming out to see Skywatch Live! with me. My name's Nathan, and I'll be your night sky tour guide today."

Nathan had a pleasant voice, confident but not too rough. Emma thought he sounded like he had a sense of humor that he wasn't quite ready to share with the audience yet. Then she thought she shouldn't be thinking about this strange man's voice at all and tried her best to focus on the stars.

"Later on tonight, you'll probably be able to see Saturn even with all of the city lights. Do you want to hear a bad joke about Saturn?" A smattering of people in the audience cheered him on. "Okay, don't hate me for this. Why does Saturn have rings?"

"Why?" the audience, including Auntie Willa, happily asked.

"Because God liked it so he put a ring on it! Saturn is not a single lady."

He was met with a mixture of laughter and groans from the audience. Emma didn't really understand the joke but she found herself laughing anyways. There was something about the way Nathan said his joke was bad that made her feel like he actually thought the opposite. She could tell by his voice that he amused himself and she couldn't help but feel endeared by that.

"I told you it was terrible! Let's move on. I'm embarrassed," Nathan continued, but Emma knew he wasn't.

Emma tried as she might to focus on the show but Nathan's voice kept drawing her in. She wanted to know more things about him; what he looked like, if he liked Chinese food, did he want to hold her hand. Her cheeks flushed at that thought. He didn't even know she was in the same room as him, let alone if he'd be interested in that. More than that, she didn't even know who he was really, just the sound of his voice. Just as she began to talk herself out of these feelings for Nathan, he concluded the show and told everyone to come see him if they had any questions about the show. This chance to talk to him face-to-face squashed all of the doubts in her mind as she scrambled to think of a question.

"Auntie Willa, I've got a question for Nathan. Do you mind if we stop and ask?"

Auntie Willa had a hunch about Emma's true intentions.

"Sure thing. I actually have to use the ladies' so how about we meet by the sun when you're through?"

"Great, thanks!" Emma replied before speeding away full of nervous energy.

Emma tried to slow down to give herself time to think of the perfect question but before she knew it she was standing in front of a tall brunette man with a kind face and a nametag that said "Nathan."

"Hey!" he greeted her, "Did you enjoy the show? Gotta question for me?"

Emma nodded and asked the first thing that came into her mind, "Why was your joke funny?"

Nathan was not expecting this question, but he hid his surprise behind an understanding smile.

"The joke about Saturn? It was a reference to a Beyonce song where she talks about some guy who wouldn't marry her. So, I guess the joke's funny for that reason, but also can you imagine God marrying a planet?" This made him laugh, but only confused Emma.

"Who's Beyonce?"

"Who's Beyonce? What are you, an alien?" he replied incredulously, but not unkindly.

Emma picked up on his playfulness and said, "No, at least I don't think so. I grew up out in the country where there isn't much music except for in church. I guess that might as well be another planet compared to here."

It turned out more than just his own jokes could make Nathan laugh. He let out a whoop and wasn't shy about it or his feelings.

'I like you!" he said, "What's your name?"

"Emma," she replied, her signature blush swept across he face, but the traditional shyness that usually came along with it wasn't there. In fact, she had never felt more confident. Against all odds, and especially against her own rules for herself, she liked him too. She felt a small pang of worry about what consequences she might face for these feelings, but she pushed them away at least for this moment.

Nathan stuck his hand out in front of him and said, "Nice to meet you, Emma. You already know my name, but would you like to know more about me?"

"Absolutely," she said as she excitedly shook his hand. This was the first thing she felt confident of since she got here. It was only after giving Nathan Auntie Willa's phone number that she realized they had held hands, and in that moment she felt more alive than any day she had back home. Emma was in love and terrified.

***

Emma didn't have to wait long by the phone before Nathan called. She and Auntie Willa talked about him that night after they got home from the planetarium. She was excited for Emma, but warned her not to get her hopes to high about some guy she just met. Emma wanted to explain that he was more than that, but didn't know how to put it into words. She was having a hard time understanding these feelings herself. Luckily, Auntie Willa was a young girl in love once, too, and understood that sometimes these things need to run their course.

"Hey! Is this Emma from the planetarium?"

Emma had made sure that Auntie Willa gave her a complete lesson on how to use the phone well before she actually had to answer it.

"It is! Is this Nathan, also from the planetarium?"

"Sure is. Now let me get straight to the point, because I'm sure you've heard enough of my disembodied voice. I want to take you to dinner. Do you eat on your planet?"

Emma couldn't help but giggle girlishly.

"Yes, of course we eat!"

"Perfect. I'll come by your place around six. I'm thinking it's about time you tried classic Chicago deep dish pizza."

"We definitely don't have that where I'm from, but it sounds great!"

"See you then, then. Buh-bye Emma."

"Goodbye!"

Emma couldn't believe what she was about to do. In her wildest dreams back home she never thought she would be going on a date with a man in the city, let alone enjoy it. Auntie Willa was right. Chicago was changing her and it was starting to become difficult not to think it's for the better.

***

Nathan took Emma on a handful more dates over the next few weeks before they finally came back to the planetarium. In that time she had learned his favorite color (red), how many siblings he had (two), his favorite book (A Brief History of Time), and he learned all that and more about her (sky blue, one, The Bible). But she couldn't help but feel that he was keeping something from her. He was almost unnervingly forthright with her, to the point where she felt like she could ask him anything, but when she asked why he worked at the planetarium he grew solemn. This only lasted a moment before he coolly replied, "because I love teaching people about space!" but she could tell that wasn't the real answer. It made her uncomfortable that she knew there was something Nathan was actively keeping from her, but she was so happily in love that she didn't want to push him away by prying.

At the planetarium, Nathan had arranged a private, after hours tour for the two of them. This was the first time she had been alone with him and that made her nervous, but excited. Nathan had been nothing but a gentleman to her the entire time they were dating. He could tell she had some reservations about becoming physical with him, and he respected that. They often held hands in the park and always hugged goodbye when he dropped her off at home, but had yet to kiss. He knew about her religion and the fact that she was only here for a couple more weeks, but every time she anxiously brought up the fact that their relationship had an expiration date he just held her close and told her not to worry about anything but that exact moment. Each time he held her, Emma could never see the sad smile Nathan had on his face.

They made the same rounds through the exhibits as Emma and Auntie Willa did the first time she came here, but this time there was no one else around and Nathan told her secrets about different artifacts on display. She loved every second of it, but couldn't help wondering about the one secret that he wouldn't share with her.

Eventually they made their way to the same theater where they first met. A starry sky was projected above them and on the floor at the front of the theater Nathan had arranged a romantic picnic, complete with different cheese, candles, and a bottle of champagne. Emma was so overwhelmed at the sight of this gesture that she kissed him right there in the doorway. She hadn't planned to, but her nervousness slipped out of her body the moment Nathan's lips touched hers. They were as soft as down, but the pressure he put behind them made it seem like they might never part. Nathan softly grabbed the back of Emma's neck with one hand and held her waist with the other. She instinctively wrapped her arms around his neck and pulled his body as close to hers as she could without fusing them together.

This kiss was like seeing the city for the first time. It was like the first bite of Chinese food. It was lying on the grass looking at the stars. It was sunrise.

When they finally parted she could see that Nathan was silently crying.

"Nathan! What's wrong? Should I not have done that?"

"No!" he said chuckling through the tears, "You definitely should have done that." He sighed and touched her cheek. "I've got to tell you something. Will you sit down with me?"

Emma felt a knot in her stomach as Nathan lead her to the blanket surrounded by candles. He popped open the champagne, poured them both a glass, and said, "You're beautiful."

"Is that what you had to tell me?"

"It's one thing, but it's not the thing."

The way he said "the thing" made it sound like some sort of storybook monster.

"Just tell me. You're making me nervous."

"Emma... I'm dying. Like, really, incurably, probably quickly dying."

Emma couldn't say anything. At first, she thought this was just another of his bad jokes but it became clear by the tears welling in his eyes that he was serious. She threw herself into his lap and cried with him, spilling the champagne onto the blanket. They held each other quietly for a while before Emma finally spoke.

"I love you."

"I love you, too"

In that moment nothing else mattered to Emma. Her home, her family, God were all forgotten as she lay there on the floor with this surprising man that wasn't even supposed to be a part of her life. Now he felt like a permanent fixture. That night she decided she could ask for forgiveness later. They had found somehow each other in an infinite universe and that was a gift more precious and unique than any other. They made love in the theater that night under the stars.

***

Emma stayed in the city just long enough to go to Nathan's funeral. She wore a simple black dress that Auntie Willa lent her. The funeral was held in a Catholic church filled with ornamentation, extravagant robes, and subdued singing. She couldn't help but feel that Nathan would have wanted something simpler, more light hearted, but who was she to say? Her first love had come and gone like a comet. She broke her own rules, as well as God's and had nothing left to show for it. When the priest called everyone up to take communion, Emma just shook her head and cried. He understood, said a blessing over her, and sent her back to her seat. She didn't understand the tradition, but felt oddly comforted by it.

When she got back to Auntie Willa's she couldn't talk at all. Emma went straight to bed and shut the door. Tomorrow she was supposed to return home. She lay awake in bed for hours thinking about if that's what she really wanted after all. Around five in the morning she gave up trying to sleep and started to pack. She left the blinds open that night and soon her room was filled with pink and orange light. The sun rising over Lake Michigan painted the sky and made the water look like light. She watched the top of the sun peek over the horizon and slowly fill the sky. "This is a new beginning," she reminded herself, "Not just for me, but for Nathan, too."

The sight of something so familiar, but all together new gave Emma the answers she needed. Looking out over the painted lake, she knew she would be okay.

END

9 798224 116485